"THAT'S ME," SAID THE MAN IN THE WHITE DUSTER.

Then he was staring into the unwinking twin muzzles of a sawed-off ten-gauge Greener as the lawman he'd taken for a rural postmaster told him not unkindly, "That ain't the plain truth, no offense. Your name's Garth MacMillan and I am arresting you in the name of the law for every charge but giggling in church."

Then the always primed and loaded MacMillan was displaying the deadly speed he was noted for as he crawfished backward, going for the guns under his open duster.

He was fast as spit on a hot stove. But that wasn't fast enough to turn the tables on a fast-enough lawman who knew MacMillan's rep and had the drop on him. So the big Greener roared and Garth MacMillan crashed backward to tear the door off its hinges with eighteen ball of double-aught buck where his belt buckle had just been.

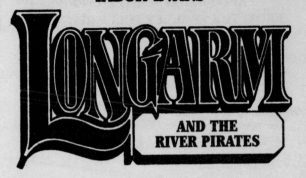

TABOR EVANS

LONGARM

AND THE RIVER PIRATES

JOVE BOOKS, NEW YORK

LONGARM AND THE RIVER PIRATES

A Jove Book / published by arrangement with
the author

PRINTING HISTORY
Jove edition / August 1998

The Penguin Putnam Inc. World Wide Web site address is
http://www.penguinputnam.com

ISBN: 0-515-12340-4

A JOVE BOOK®
Jove Books are published by The Berkley Publishing Group,
a member of Penguin Putnam Inc.,
200 Madison Avenue, New York, New York 10016.
JOVE and the "J" design are trademarks
belonging to Jove Publications, Inc.

PRINTED IN THE UNITED STATES OF AMERICA

10 9 8 7 6 5 4 3 2 1

LONGARM

AND THE RIVER PIRATES

Chapter 1

The crossroads settlement of Aurora baked on treeless rolling prairie an easy ride east of Denver, Colorado. The modest whitewashed post office stood back from the dusty coach road without a lick of other cover within pistol range of the one front door. The shifty-eyed rider in the ankle-length white duster was considering things such as concealed pistoleers as he dismounted from his black livery nag out front and tethered it loosely to the hitching rail.

He wore his duster unbuttoned over a pair of concealed Schofield .45s. He paused on the post office steps to study the sunbaked dust all around from the deep shade of his foursquare Stetson before he nodded grimly to nobody at all and went on in.

He didn't glance at any of the wanted posters on the post office wall. He'd taken a good look at his own face in the mirror the last time he'd shaved. There was nobody else on his side of the counter. A tall dark cuss wearing a green eyeshade and wire-framed specs was sorting mail on the far side of the counter. The newcomer could see there was nobody else back there in the simple one-room rural mail drop. He moseyed over to the counter to say, "Howdy. What happened to the redheaded gal they had working here?"

1

The man said, "She got married. So I was 'pointed to take her place."

The first part of that statement was true. The second was a barefaced lie. But the man, who'd come for any mail addressed to his false identity in care of General Delivery, Aurora, Colorado, lied just as baldly when he said, "I'd be D. W. Weddington off the Diamond K and I'm expecting a letter in care of General Delivery here."

The taller man behind the counter started to shake his head, then brightened and said, "I might have sorted out something like that. The outfit's brand sticks in my mind. D. W. Weddington, you say, expecting a letter from Waco, Texas?"

"That's me," said the man in the white duster expansively. Then he was staring into the unwinking twin muzzles of a sawed-off ten-gauge Greener as the lawman he'd taken for a rural postmaster told him not unkindly, "That ain't the plain truth, no offense. Your name's Garth MacMillan and I am arresting you in the name of the law on every charge but giggling in church."

Then the always primed and loaded Garth MacMillan was displaying the deady speed he was noted for as he crawfished backward, going for the guns under his open duster.

He was fast as spit on a hot stove. But that wasn't fast enough to turn the tables on a fast-enough lawman who knew MacMillan's rep and had the drop on him. So the big Greener roared and Garth MacMillan crashed backward to tear the door off its hinges with eighteen balls of double-aught buck where his belt buckle had just been.

As he sprawled out in the dooryard to stare up at the sun through swirls of gunsmoke and 'dobe dust, the taller man who'd blasted him at point-blank range stepped outside to join him, holding a double-action Colt .44-40 in place of the shotgun he'd emptied into MacMillan as he hunkered down by the dying killer to remark in a conversational tone, "You shouldn't have done that. I'd be U.S. Deputy Mar-

2

shal Custis Long of the Denver District Court in case you're wondering who just killed you. I'd be proud to write to your true love in Waco and tell her where we buried you if you'd care to discuss the contents of that strongbox you rode off with from the Overland Stage south of Julesburg.''

MacMillan smiled up gamely and replied, ''I've heard of you. Tell all my pals nobody less than the one and original Longarm could have tricked this child to an early grave. I can see I ain't got much use for the proceeds of that last robbery. But what will you give me in exchange for its present whereabouts?''

A young kid in bib overalls was peeking at them around the corner of the barn across the way. Longarm called out for the kid to fetch the town midwife before he turned back to the dying road agent and quietly asked, ''What are you asking for, other than a cure?''

MacMillan groaned, ''Tell me who peached on me! I know I won't be able to pay the son of a bitch back. But I'd hate to cash in my last chips not knowing who to suspect the most.''

Longarm said, ''It wasn't Miss Carmencita down Waco way, if that gives you any comfort, old son.''

The gutshot but shock-numbed rider of the owlhoot trail sighed and said, ''Them words comfort me more than my words can say, Longarm. But Carmencita was the only one writing to me in care of this dinky town. Nobody else I ever rode with knew I was picking up my mail here in Aurora, right?''

Longarm gently answered. ''Wrong. You'd ridden far and you'd changed your name more than once along the way. But Miss Carmencita went on dancing the fandango at that same establishment where the two of you were known so well. Seeing she hardly gets any letters in English from her native land, it was easy to guess who was sending her postal money orders signed D. W. Weddington, care of the G.P.O. Aurora. When I asked that redhead you mentioned about you, and she said you'd said you'd ridden for

3

the Diamond K in these parts, I just had to ride out this way and meet you personally. You see, Tex, the Diamond K is a good piece off to the southwest of here, on the Camp Weld road, and their ramrod is a pal of mine who never heard of any D. W. Weddington. So about the loot from that last robbery . . ."

But the sneaky Garth MacMillan remained sneaky to the last, and the fat old gal who came back with the kid, and was holding wet and dry towels in the unlikely event they'd do any good, hunkered down by Longarm to feel the outlaw's pulse and excuse him from having so little to say.

But there was more than one way to skin a cat, or trace a livery nag back to its registered owner by its brand. So late that evening the landlady of a boardinghouse near a certain Denver livery stable said she'd be proud to let Longarm and his pals look around, as long as they didn't bust her property up. But the boarder she'd known as D. W. Weddington had already done so.

It was the keen-eyed Deputy Smiley, said to be part Pawnee, who spotted a tiny crumb of plaster against the baseboard behind a bed table, and thought to look behind a Currier and Ives rendition of a steamboat race on the moonlit Mississippi. Weddington cum MacMillan had punched a sizeable hole in the plaster and lath behind the print to bank a canvas money bag. The bag was more than half empty by that time, but a third of the loot recovered beat none of the loot recovered, so what the hell.

Thus, next morning when he reported to work almost on time at the Denver Federal Building, wearing a fresh shirt with his shoestring tie under the tobacco-tweed suit they'd been making him wear in town since President Hayes had won on a draconian reform ticket, Longarm expected to be congratulated on a job well done.

But as Mr. Robert Burns had observed so well, the best-laid plans of mice and men were inclined to get all fucked up. So Longarm's boss, Marshal Billy Vail, began the pro-

4

ceedings in his oak-lined inner office by cussing Longarm out for killing the deadly Garth MacMillan.

Billy Vail had never in living memory invited Longarm to sit down on his own side of the cluttered desk. So Longarm helped himself to a seat in the one leather guest chair, and broke out one of his own three-for-a-nickel cheroots in self-defense as his older, shorter, and dumpier boss puffed on an expensive but dreadful-smelling cigar.

Longarm let Billy Vail wait until he had his own smoke going, and his own thoughts back on track, before he asked in as mild a tone as he could manage, "Have you gone out of your fucking head, Billy Vail? You warned me MacMillan was dangerous beyond common self-preservation. You warned me he'd slapped leather and won over lawmen who'd had the drop on him in the past. You warned me true. The two of us were closer to one another across that post office counter than you and me are right now across this desk. I waited till I had the drop on him with that post office Greener before I declared any hostile intent, and it was still too close for comfort. He went for his guns. Both of them. What was I supposed to have done about that, drop the shotgun and whip out my dick?"

Vail grumbled, "You didn't have to blow him out the door to die on the damned street with the whole town watching, albeit from behind a heap of lace curtains. The *Denver Post* and *Rocky Mountain News* printed extras and you're on the dad-blasted front pages again."

Longarm blew a modest smoke ring and calmly replied, "That's fair. I was the one who brought the son of a bitch to justice with a modest amount of double-aught buck. What's got into you this morning, boss? *I'm* the one they'll be pestering for autographs and such."

Billy Vail shook his balding bullet head and grimly replied, "No, you won't. I don't want you available for comment at the inquest. If you ain't there you won't be able to tell anyone how we tracked the late Garth MacMillan down. The Postmaster General don't want anyone else to know

5

hòw we did it. They're already having trouble over the contractural obligations implied by the sale and purchase of a U.S. stamp, to say nothing of a postal money order.''

Longarm shrugged, flicked ash on the rug because Billy Vail seemed unable or unwilling to provide a damned ashtray, and asked, "How can MacMillan's lawyers bring up the prick's civil rights at this late date?''

Vail said, "MacMillan's lawyers ain't the problem. John Wesley Hardin is the problem.''

Longarm snorted incredulously and decided, "I was right. You've gone out of your fucking head this morning. I remember that preacher's son gone bad from Abilene, before they shut down the Bull's Head Tavern. He was mean as hell. But he ain't been mean to anybody since they sent him to Huntsville Prison back in '77, has he?''

Vail answered soberly, "He has. Being educated, at least for a murderous tinhorn, John Wesley has been studying the law by mail order to while away his time in durance vile. They say he has the makings of a lawyer. He's sure been arguing law a heap of late.''

Longarm grimaced and said, "I always knew that boy would end up a really vicious son of a bitch. A lawyer with his natural mean streak is not to be contemplated lightly. But what's all this have to do with my shooting MacMillan and recovering what was left of that money he rode off with?''

Vail sighed and said, "The Texas Rangers tracked John Wesley Hardin all the way to Pollard, Alabama, much the same way. In that case it was not the fugitive writing to a known associate. Hardin was living as an Alabama timber merchant with his wife, Jane Hardin née Bowan from Coon Hollow, Texas. *She* was the one who kept writing home to her own kith and kin. A Texas bloodhound, Ranger Captain Armstrong, had outstanding warrants to spare on the dutiful daughter's mean man. So after a mess of letters postmarked Pollard, Alabama, made their way to Hardin's in-laws,

6

Armstrong and his backup made their way to Pollard and arrested the son of a bitch.''

Longarm grinned and said, ''The army catches heaps of deserters the same way. They ask for your home address when you sign up for a five-year hitch. I reckon kids dumb enough to desert ain't smart enough to see the army might have their home address on file.''

Vail said, ''Pay attention. John Wesley Hardin ain't about to desert the U.S. Army. He wants out of Huntsville Prison. So he's filed him a petition, acting as his own attorney, allowing the U.S. Government had no right to invade his privacy by telling others where his woman was writing home from. He says she paid good money for each and every one of them stamps, with the implied contract being said stamps entitled her to private messages home, not to any Texas Rangers.''

Longarm frowned thoughtfully and asked, ''Does that mean we don't have the right to track a white outlaw across an Indian reserve, the implied contract being such range is reserved for Indian riders?''

Vail scowled and said, ''The Postmaster General and me agree they never said toad squat about postage stamps when they wrote the Bill of Rights. All the shit they left *out* has been a boon to lawyers ever since. John Wesley Hardin was sentenced to twenty-five at hard, and he was cardhouse lucky they didn't make him to the rope dance. We don't want him out any sooner. We don't want him, or any other jailhouse lawyer, reading about the way you tracked Garth MacMillan to a crossroads post office via the U.S. mails. So you just ain't going to be available as a witness down the hall when they hold a public hearing on the gunning of a miserable gunslinger.''

Vail exhaled an expansive cloud of pungent smoke and added, ''We can let the reporters talk to that midwife you enlisted to take the dying desperado's pulse. We can let them talk to any and all of the good citizens of Aurora who now swear they watched the whole fight. We just don't

7

want any reporters talking to *you,* or taking notes as you testify in your infernal unvarnished way."

Longarm leaned back in the leather chair and declared, "Well, it's fine riding weather along the Front Range and this old pal of mine has been pestering me to tag along on a mine inspection tour."

But Vail growled, "The taxpapers of These United States do not pay you to go riding with pretty mine owners. I said I wanted you out of town, not having fun. So I'm loaning you to an old pal who wears the same badge as me out California way. He's bought himself one of those Chinese puzzles you can't put together until you figure out which of the parts is the key."

Longarm asked, "Don't you mean you can't take *apart*? I've seen such puzzles in Chinese notions shops."

Vail sighed and said, "I wish you wouldn't correct your elders. I said put together because the pieces seem scattered all up and down the Sacramento River from the Mother Lode to the Frisco Bay. None of my old pal's deputies know shit about Chinese puzzles and so, seeing you're such an expert on them Chinese twangs and meat cleavers . . ."

"That's *tongs* and *hatchet men*," Longarm stated, adding modestly, "and besides, I know more French than Chinese, and I ain't sure I know enough French to get laid."

Vail snapped, "Everybody knows enough French to get laid, and you get along better with Chinamen and Indians than some deem wholesome. So you can read the letter I got from my old sidekick as you wend your way west to give him a hand with his Chinese puzzle. For as the Indian chief said, I have spoken."

Chapter 2

Longarm traveled as light as possible. But the West Coast lay a smart ways off. So the possibles lashed to his Mc-Clellan saddle, along with his Winchester '73, weighed more than the army saddle itself, and it was just as well there was an open slot running the length of the saddle's seat.

The American adaptation of an Austro-Hungarian cavalry saddle was ventilated that way for the comfort of the horse. A man who knew how to ride a horse was supposed to be smart enough to keep his balls out of the slot. Longarm rode in tight pants, and found the central slot a swell hand grip when he had to tote such a load on and off trains.

Old Henry, the young squirt who played the office typewriter, had routed him west with as few railroad transfers as practical. So Longarm read Henry's typed carbon transcript of the West Coast cry for help more than once as he traveled north to Cheyenne by day-tripper.

He could see why Marshal Tavish Seaforth of the Sacramento Delta District needed help with the sudden increase in blood and slaughter among the normally peacable Sons of Han. But Longarm had been trying to tell Billy Vail the pure truth when he'd allowed he didn't know too much about Chinamen. He'd had to stand for law, order, and fair play during those recent race riots inspired by the Chinese-hating rabble-rouser Dinty Kearney, a foin broth of a boyo who meant to keep Americay for dacent be-jasus Americans and all. But while saving a Chinaman from a lynch mob, or comforting a frightened waitress from the Golden Dragon, had taught him that Chinese blood ran red and that it wasn't true what they said about Chinese women, he'd only wound up knowing a tad more than most West-by-God-Virginia boys about the fair-sized but almost invisible Chinese community of the West.

He did know enough to hope like hell they were talking about mere highbinders, or Chinese thugs, acting on their own. If the outbreak of sudden death along the Sacramento had been the work of *bu how day* or hatchet men riding for any of the half-dozen West Coast *tongs,* he was likely wasting his time as well as risking his neck.

White lawmen had caught Oriental crooks running with one of the outlaw Highbinder Societies because Chinese merchants didn't like to be robbed any more than others. But when you asked your average Son of Han about the *tong,* or neighborhood protective society he paid tribute to, you got a blank stare and a total denial that anybody in the neighborhood had ever heard the word. They also swore they'd never heard of chop suey in their old country. Longarm was willing to believe that much.

Since Chinese folks *would* turn in *regular* crooks if they robbed or hurt Chinese, it seemed likely the tong leaders were viewed as a mixture of Robin Hood and J. P. Morgan, investing funds from extortion, gambling, whoremongering, and such in honest businesses run by worthy Orientals who'd never in this world get a grubstake from any white banker.

Longarm had tangled with tong hatchet men in the past, and lived to tell about it. But it hadn't been easy. Going up against outlandish outlaws always made him feel for poor Trooper Martin, Custer's bugler at the Little Big Horn, who'd arrived on the New York docks as plain old Giovanni Martini from sunny Italy. He had somehow wound up in the U.S. Army, and found himself on the sunny slopes of Greasy Grass Ridge with Custer shouting complicated orders, in English, to be relayed over to Benteen's column, or maybe Reno's. All Trooper Martin would ever be sure about was that Custer had sent him for help, at the last minute, so that *he*, at least, had come off that ridge alive.

Putting the fool dispatches away as he puffed in the smoking car, Longarm tried to recall the six tongs in Frisco alone that you couldn't get any Chinese to talk about. One Daughter of Han who ran a fan-tan palace for a tong she wouldn't come right out and name had confided that the Frisco Bay tongs were *Bik Kong, Hip Sing, Yun Ying, Sen Suey King, Suey Ong,* and *Suey Sing.* He'd confided in his own official report that he hadn't been dead certain she hadn't recited a Chinese menu to him. Others he'd be-friended during the riots had told him, or warned him, that the *Ong Leongs* were "belly biggee" along the rail lines all the way east. He *did* know none of the true tongs went in for random killings. So he could only hope those Oriental bodies bobbing in the Sacramento of late had been tossed in by some vicious criminal. For vicious crimes got solved all the time. But nobody on either side of the wide Pacific had ever been able to pin a killing on a tong, or prove which tong had ordered it.

He figured he was up against *some* tong as he was changing trains in Cheyenne that afternoon. As he toted his load along the platform to board the westbound Union Pacific Flyer, he naturally got to admiring the way the Junoesque hips ahead of him swished those green velveteen skirts as their owner followed a porter wheeling a Saratoga trunk. It was going to take the Pullman sleeping car thirty-odd hours to fly the two of them many a tedious mile. So an ass that fine could make up for most any face that wasn't downright repulsive, and Longarm was content to wait until the gal got to the train steps ahead of him and had to turn naturally. Nobody loped ahead of a gal and turned to ogle back at her unless he was a total asshole who liked to scare them off.

So that was what Longarm thought of the tall drink of water in a checked suit and cowboy hat who loped past him and then the gal in green velveteen, then slowed down and ogled back at her with a shit-eating grin, declaring, "Well, I swan, and is it true what they say about gals like you?"

The gal naturally ignored him, or tried to. But as she swept past with her head held proudly and a bitty straw boater riding the crest of her pinned-up raven hair, the total asshole grabbed hold of one green sleeve to spin her around as he brayed, "Aw, don't be so stuck up. I am only trying to change your luck, you pretty little squint-eyed thing!"

That was when Longarm saw the face that went with the veleveteen skirts and Junoesque hips. That was when he figured he was up against a tong, with the tong a couple of moves ahead of him.

For while Chinese men were scattered coast to coast in the wake of the wedding of the rails, and the layoffs that had followed, Chinese *women* were scarce as hen's teeth, east or west, and neither men nor women of the ordinary Oriental persuasion had the pocket jingle for velveteen and Pullman cars. So Longarm did not move in to rescue the maiden fair from the amorous villain. It felt funny, and he couldn't look the porter in the eye as he swung wide of the ugly scene and just kept going without looking back as somebody somewhere sounded as if he was getting his face slapped pretty convincingly.

Longarm grimaced in disdain as he boarded his car, hunted down the conductor, and asked how much extra a private compartment was going to cost him. He wasn't about to face the coming night with only green canvas curtains between his reclining form and any *bu how day* roaming the aisles after dark with a hatchet or, more likely, one of those nine-shots-and-a-shotgun-blast Le Mat Duplex revolvers they seemed to favor for such chores.

The conductor knew who Longarm was, and allowed

12

they could afford to let him have a compartment for nothing extra, seeing he'd brought his Winchester along and the infernal Shoshoni were acting up again on the west slopes of the Great Divide.

So Longarm stowed his saddle and possibles in a forward compartment before he moseyed back to the club car. He was surprised to feel so little surprise when he saw that that same slant-eyed gal in green velveteen was hogging a small table to herself and a glass of birch beer, with the one chair left turned around in an inviting way.

Longarm ordered plain lager and stayed at the bar, when he found he could examine her unobserved in the tinted mirror of the back-bar. As he did so, he decided she wasn't pure Chinese. Her black hair was a mite too fine and wavy. Her cameo features didn't allow for any snap judgments. She kept turning her head to sip more of her drink or fix her sloe eyes on something outside as the train crawled out of the Cheyenne yards at an ever-increasing speed. So at some angles she looked Oriental as all get-out, while at others she could have almost passed for white. Their eyes suddenly met in the mirror and she looked quicky away. Longarm swung his eyes out a window on his side of the car and kept them there, knowing that once a gal had caught him staring at her, she was sure to try and catch him at it some more.

He didn't want to flirt with any tong spy they'd sent to find out just how much he really knew. He tried to decide his next move, knowing how subtle, or how rough, those *bu how day* of either sex could play.

He finished his beer and headed back to his compartment, braced for most anything. But nothing happened. He read a magazine he'd picked up in Cheyenne as the scenery outside got more interesting.

The Union Pacific tracks ran in the same general direction as the old wagon routes over the Rockies, but went through cuts and tunnels that hadn't been there for the wagon trains. Naturally, the Iron Horse wasn't as bound by

13

grazing and watering considerations as real livestock. So the railroad saved a lot of miles by punching its way through more dramatic scenery, and by supper time they'd gone under and over the Medicine Bow Range to steam on out across the Great Divide Basin, which was high up, but looked as if they'd dropped back down to the Nebraska prairies.

If you studied closely you could guess when you'd crossed the Continental Divide by watching whether the ditch water alongside the tracks was flowing east to the Atlantic or west to the Pacific—or so they told you in the U.P. travel folders.

As he made his way forward to the dining car, Longarm could have told anyone who asked that, in point of fact, the eastern slopes of the Rockies drained into the Gulf of Mexico, while their westernslopes this far south all drained into the Sea of Cortez or Gulf of California.

Nobody asked him. When he got to the dining car he found all the tables but one had been taken. He made his way to the last table left and sat down, with his back to the forward bulkhead.

There was something odd about the scenery outside. He was still trying to decide what it was when the waiter came to take his order. So he ordered their special of roast beef with mashed potatoes and stringbeans. Then he stared out the window some more, seeing nothing spookier than a rolling sea of tawny short grass going gold and lavender as the locomotive chased the ever-lower sun without a prayer of catching it before it sank to the west.

That Chinese or part-Chinese gal in the silly hat and green veleveteen had entered the car, glanced around for a place to settle her swell ass, and seemed to be headed his way with an uncertain expression on her exotic face.

Longarm half rose from his own seat when she demurely asked if the empty one across from him was taken. He played his own cards as poker-faced as he knew how, and if they really thought he was too stupid to notice those sloe

14

eyes and high cheekbones, so be it. A gal with as much white blood as she seemed to have might not look half as Chinese to a pure Chinese.

As she sat down she introduced herself as a Miss Natasha Godanov, and allowed she was headed for Virginia City. Longarm felt no call to lie about things they already knew. So he told her who he was and where he was going. He sweetened the pot by adding, "I've been asked to give the Delta District a hand with some sort of tong war."

"Tong war?" she asked, as if the term was new to her.

It wasn't easy. But Longarm managed not to compliment her on her acting as the waiter brought his order and took hers.

It was rude to start ahead of a lady, and he knew that the chicken she'd ordered was already made up and in their warming oven. So Longarm held his fire and just sipped ice water as he faced her in a sort of awkward silence, waiting for her to make her next move. But somebody must have told her not to talk too much, and she didn't, even though he could tell she was wishing he'd say something, anything, to get the game going.

So for openers, Longarm said, "That Indian scare must have folks in these parts really proddy."

She looked confounded and murmured, "Indian scare, Deputy Long?"

He said, "My friends call me Custis. Didn't *your* friends tell you that? The Shoshoni in these parts get to acting up every now and again. This used to be their hunting ground and some of them seem to be poor losers. The cattle outfits who've been grazing this range since the late Chief Buffalo Horn cashed in his chips must be braced for some more Shoshoni trouble."

The Oriental gal who'd given her fool self a Slavic name smiled uncertainly and said, "Didn't I read somewhere that Buffalo Horn was a chief of the Bannock tribe?"

Longarm smiled thinly and replied, "You must ride this line often. Bannock, Shoshoni, Snake, and such are what

15

we call a mess of folks who call themselves *Ho*. The nations we describe as Apache and Navaho are related too. Do you rather be called Chinee or Chinese, Miss Natasha?''

She blinked her sloe eyes, heaved a sigh, and said, ''My mother was Finnish. My father was a Russian Tatar, not *Tartar,* darn it. You are hardly the first who's ever accused me of looking Chinese. But I'm not, and to tell the truth, I'm awfully sick of explaining relatives I've never met. My late father simply looked like any other Russian. But he said I resembled one of his grandmothers, and of course some Finns have an Oriental cast to their features. God only knows why.''

Their waiter came to the table with her order. So Longarm picked up his fork at last as he said, ''I stand corrected and I'll never call you a Chinese again, Miss Natasha.''

Then she was screaming fit to bust as shattered glass rained down on their untasted meals and the waiter just stood there for one long frozen moment while a bright red stain spread across his white linen jacket. Then he was on the floor as Longarm reached across the table to grab a green sleeve and haul her away from the windows to the glass-and-blood-spattered carpeting while somebody else was shouting, ''Indians!''

It only seemed fair. For though she seemed to be a bare-faced liar, she was awfully pretty and there didn't seem to be any way she or her tong could have arranged for all those Shoshoni whooping and shooting in the tricky light outside.

Chapter 3

The war party hadn't been led by anybody smart enough to block a cut or tunnel, so the train steamed through their fusillade in next to no time, with the most serious casualty the colored waiter who'd been caught by that round passing across the table between Longarm and a gal who still looked more Chinese than Russian.

To her credit, the gal who insisted she was Natasha Godanov got right to work on their downed waiter with table linen and a finger bowel of hot water off the galley range. Meanwhile, Longarm cut the man's bloody white jacket and undershirt away with a steak knife. They'd told him tongs were mutual-aid societies, and old Natasha had the bleeding stopped, on the outside leastways, by the time the conductor joined them.

The conductor nodded grimly at Longarm and said, *"Told* you we'd heard there might be Indian trouble. There's others hurt back in the coach cars. But we dasn't stop this side of Bitter Creek. How bad does it look for young Cato here, ma'am?"

Natasha answered with her sad sloe eyes because the young waiter had opened his own eyes, murmuring, "Don't whup me, Momma! I's sorry I took them pins from your sewing basket to go fishing, and do you make this bellyache go 'way I won't never do it no more, hear?''

Natasha turned to Longarm and quietly told him, "We need some medicine. Anything a hundred proof will do."

The conductor said something about not giving a gutshot man anything to drink. But Longarm had already risen to duck into the galley and yell, "We need some of that brandy you flame them crappy Susans with!"

The colored chef asked if he meant crêpes suzettes, and Longarm got what he wanted quickly by roaring, "Give me the fucking brandy and I don't care *how* you spell crappy Susan!"

Rejoining the conductor and the girl as they knelt beside a dying waiter, Longarm held the bottle to Cato's lips and said, "Have some of this belly-soothing and try not to breath so deep, old son."

Cato sobbed, "It hurts so bad I want to die, but I don't *want* to die, Captain!"

Longarm insisted, "Sip some of this and you have my word you won't ever have to howdy Mr. Death, Cato."

"You promise, Captain?" asked the dying youth in a hopeful tone.

Longarm promised. The dying waiter took a good swig on the bottle, coughed, laughed, and went limp as a dishrag with his head on Natasha's knees.

The conductor said, "Well, I reckon a white lie told in kindness don't count."

Longarm said, "I never lied to him. He ain't the first man I've had that conversation with. It's only us *living* folks who ever meet up with Mr. Death. We see him, or think we see him, in the eyes of dead folks. But dead folks don't see *nothing*. They don't know they're dead. So it ain't the dead who fear death. They *can't* fear death as much as the living, see?"

The conductor rose to his feet, sternly telling the other crew members to tidy up and get back to work, declaring, "I want everything normal as we can manage by the time

18

we stop at Bitter Creek to take the dead and wounded off, hear?''

Longarm got to his own feet, asking how long they'd likely be in the jerkwater high-country town, seeing he had others waiting for him out California way.

The conductor said they'd go on from Bitter Creek when the Union Pacific and War Department, in that order, said it would be safe to go on.

Longarm didn't want a lecture on railroading through Indian trouble. So he let the older man grump off. Then he hunkered back down to tell the gal, ''You may as well put his head on the floor now, Miss Natasha. You've already got blood on your skirts and we'd better take some ice water to it before it dries.''

She seemed to be quietly crying as he helped her to her feet. He'd forgotten who she likely was and what an actress she had to be in all the excitement. The other diners had all cleared out by then. So he got her down to a far table and told her to spread the stained part of her velveteen skirt over a corner of the table as she sat down.

''That would mean sitting with my unmentionables on the seat and my limbs exposed, sir!'' she protested.

He said, ''Everything you'd as soon keep hidden will still be out of sight behind the tablecloth, Miss Natasha. It's *your* green velveteen. I know I'd sure want to run some ice water through this brown tweed I got on if it was soaked with fresh blood.''

So she hoisted her skirts waist-high as she set her shapely rump down, and Longarm helped her spread the stained folds on the tabletop before he told her to hold it like that while he got the blood out.

As he sat across from her with a pitcher of ice water and some wet napkins, she asked him where he'd learned so much about bloodstains.

He said, ''They held a war one time and I was invited. I've seen some bleeding since, riding for the law. After you've tried everything on bloodstains, you see there's only

19

one thing better than cold water, and that's peroxide, which we ain't got.''

She asked if he was talking about hydrogen peroxide. When he asked if there was any other kind, she said she had some in her Saratoga trunk, which just so happened to be in her own compartment. Longarm knew gals traveling alone had all sorts of stuff, and he didn't see how in thunder the most diabolical Oriental could have planned on an Indian ambush and a bloodstained skirt. But he still said, "I'd as soon stick with ice water, and if you want to go to any private Pullman compartment with this child, it will have to be the one I know a heap better, no offense.''

She looked bewildered and asked, "Have I said something to offend you, Custis? You keep making the oddest comments, just when I think I've begun to understand you.''

He saw he was making some progress, the blood being fresh and the water being cold as it soaked through the velveteen into the rolled napkin below. He smiled thinly and said, "Oh, I'm sure you understand more about me than I understand about you, ma'am. Our meeting up like this was pure coincidence, right?''

She said, "I don't know what you're talking about. I told you who I was and that I was on my way to Virginia City. If you must know, I have been living by my wits in Deadwood and I heard Madame Mustache was in need of a faro dealer in Virginia City.''

"Simone Jules ain't with us no more,'' Longarm said. "Last I heard, she'd cashed in her chips in Bodie with a swig of cyanide.''

It didn't work. The gal who called herself Natasha and claimed to know how to deal faro gasped, "Madame Mustache is dead? In Bodie and not Virginia City? When did all this happen?''

Longarm said, "Recently. You really knew her true name, didn't you. The way I heard it, she wasn't getting any younger, and a pair of tinhorns had busted her faro bank on her along about last September. I reckon she was too depressed to spend the coming winter broke, alone, and feeling old. They say she wasn't yet fifty, but she'd led a hard life. Did you know Jane Cannary up in Deadwood, speaking of aging prematurely?''

Natasha said, "Calamity Jane was the one who told me Madame Mustache was doing so well in Virginia City. She said they'd worked together in more than one mining camp, with the Madame using the name Dumont.''

"You're good," Longarm told her, scrubbing over a spot that looked fairly clean as he talked softly above the clicking of the wheels below them. "You don't act Chinese, you don't dress Chinese, and you surely don't *talk* Chinese. I don't suppose you ever heard of Little Pete out Frisco way?''

She said she hadn't, and asked who he was talking about.

Longarm said, "His Chinese name sounds like it deserves to be served with fried noodles. But as if you didn't know, Little Pete is a member of the Gin Sin Seer gang. They say he's too disrespectful of his elders to be invited into any of the respectable tongs. My point is that the mean little cuss was brought up in Frisco, and he looks and acts so American it makes the other opium pushers and fan-tan dealers sick. It ain't true all heathen Chinese wear blue pajamas and talk funny.''

She said her skirt looked as clean as he was likely to manage, and pulled it modestly down over her thighs as she added, "There you go talking funny about Chinese again. What are we going to do about that poor waiter up at the other end of the car?''

He said, "Nothing. We've done all we could for him and the rest is up to the train crew. We'll be pulling into Bitter Creek in a while. We'll be laying over, and I know they have a Western Union there if you want to tell your tong I'm on to you.''

She blazed, "What on earth are you talking about? I'm . . . All right, I'm sometimes known as Tiger Tasha, a pro-

21

fessional gambler. I'm thrice married to brutes, but never in this world a whore. I told you truly who I was, where I've come from, and where I'm going. What more can I possibly say?"

Longarm replied, "Nothing. Anything is possible, but I've learned to bet my money on the easy answers, and it ain't as easy to accept a fellow traveler who just happens to look Chinese falling in with me as I head west to look into Chinese matters."

The conductor came back in with a railroad detective Longarm knew well enough to nod to. The conductor said, "We're going to have to open this dining car up again or commence to pass sandwiches back to famished passengers who missed their suppers. I don't think they'll wait until we roll into Bitter Creek this evening, durn those pesky Shoshoni!"

Longarm got up from the table, saying, "Me and Miss Natasha first. The dead waiter up to the other end had just brought our orders when the first round came through the windows."

He turned to the sloe-eyed brunette to ask if ham and cheese on rye sounded right. "I fear they don't serve egg fu yung."

She said something dreadful about his mother. He ambled into the galley and got them some sandwiches anyway.

Rejoining her, he said, "I have running water and a bottle of Maryland rye in my compartment, Miss Natasha. What say we eat and compare notes back yonder? I'll tell you everything I know, because I don't know toad squat, but you have me guessing and we might be able to make a deal with your tong, if I'm guessing right about why they sent you."

She swore in what sounded like Russian, but got up to tag along as she added, "I'm starved and I could certainly use a stiff drink, you suspicious son of a bitch."

As he led her out of the dining car he quietly told her, "That's twice. I know you're a woman and I ain't allowed

22

to bust your nose for insulting my poor momma, Miss Natasha. But don't do that again if you want me to talk nice to you.''

She marveled, ''You call it talking nice to accuse a girl of being a lying breed of some sort who's been plotting against you with some Chinese *twang*?''

He chuckled and said, ''That was a nice touch. I'm guessing you had orders to just see what I might know. Had they meant me more harm than that, they'd have sent somebody like Little Pete. So I'm guessing the Chinese victims my California pals have been hauling out of the river betwixt Sacramento and the Frisco Bay must have been under the protection of your tong. Had they been the intended victims of tong hatchet men, or had tong hatchet men known just who was doing what to whom, there'd have been no need for them to have you pump me.''

''You're crazy!'' she insisted as they traversed a narrow corridor in semi-privacy. Between cars she added, ''How many times do I have to tell you I'm the Tiger Tasha of honest repute in many a mining camp?''

To which Longarm modestly replied, ''I've passed through many a mining camp and bucked many a tiger my ownself. So I reckon it's just a coincidence we've never heard tell of one another, right?''

She almost fell against him as the deck beneath them shifted an unexpected way. But he didn't have to let go of the sandwiches as she gracefully regained her balance, saying sheepishly, ''Of course I knew who *you* were right off. I told you I'd been talking to Calamity Jane, and all right, I was out to pick you up and find out if half of what she told me about you could be true.''

Caught off guard, Longarm protested, ''I never! Not with Calamity Jane Cannary! I don't suppose she told you why the boys all call her a calamity?''

Natasha laughed wickedly, but demurely replied, ''I don't see how she could have picked up that many social diseases without dying. I never said I believed you fought

23

it out with Wild Bill for her favors. Do you believe me now about my being who I said I was?''

He didn't. But a man sitting in with a piss-poor hand always had the chance of drawing an ace, or a slip of the tongue, if he just kept bluffing with the cards he had. So he told her, ''They say Little Pete knows all the gossip about society swells up on Nob Hill, seeing he speaks good English and pays attention to matters outside his own part of Chinatown. But it don't cut no ice either way. I said I meant to tell you all I knew about the tong war or whatever, and yonder's the door to my compartment.''

She slid the door open and stepped through as the train suddenly slowed and threw him off balance. He staggered back along the aisle a piece, recovered, and forged on after her, muttering, ''We're either coming in to Bitter Creek or under attack again.''

Then he'd joined her in the privacy of his compartment to see by the one dim bulkhead fixture that she'd tossed her hat on the berth and seemed to be shucking her green velveteen and silk chemise over her head in one astoundingly supple motion. He could see he'd been right about her Junoesque behind, because she'd been wearing nothing else but her green-gartered mesh-stockings and high-button shoes.

As she turned with a roguish smile and a twinkle in her big slanty eyes, he saw she was built just as well down her naked front as well.

He shut the door behind him with a boot heel and held out one of the sandwiches as she calmly asked, ''Do you see any concealed weapons you have to worry about, Custis?''

To which he could only reply, ''Not hardly. But I ought to know better and I sure wish I did.''

Then he asked her to hold both sandwiches while he got out of his own infernal hardware, boots, and duds.

Chapter 4

Longarm was glad he'd drawn the green canvas blinds in his compartment before he'd gone to supper. They were going at it by lamplight dog-style when their train pulled into Bitter Creek and hissed to a shuddering stop.

So he was enjoying a private viewing of her broad but shapely derriere as his old organ-grinder slid in and out between her smooth ivory buttocks. But he realized again that it wasn't true what they said about Chinese gals, and all her uncommonly wet and cozy ring-dang-do could tell him was that she seemed to be enjoying it as much as she said she was.

As he rolled her on her back to finish in her right again, the Oriental-looking gal who claimed she wasn't asked what all those shouts and boot crunches just outside the window blinds might mean.

He kept moving in her, as most men would have at such a time, but told her, "It's likely just the pointless scurry that goes with your average Indian scare. By this time the young bucks who smoked up a passing train have doubtless headed for home to count coup and blow their nose flutes at admiring young ladies. But nobody moves a train down a dark track with Indians on the prowl before they can send a hand-car ahead to make sure of the tracks and a mounted patrol to make sure the tracks stay that way. Could we just screw some more and talk later? I don't know about you, but I'm fixing to come.''

She moaned that that made two of them as she began to gyrate her big old hips like a whore who'd married a rich mining man for his money and wanted him to die young.

Longarm didn't care whether she was conning him with her cunt or not. It felt just grand, and if Billy Vail ever found out about this, Longarm was going to plead line of duty. He'd established that she hadn't been sent to assassinate him. It seemed highly unlikely they were ever going to call her as a federal witness against anybody, and he wasn't going to get anything out of her by spurning her sassy approach.

So he just let go for the moment, and felt it all the way down to his toes when he shot another wad in her quivering wet innards.

As she hugged him lovingly with all four limbs, the naturally warm-natured or mighty dramatic gal sobbed, ''Oh, that was lovely! How I wish it could just go on and on and on forever!''

Longarm kissed her smooth throat and said, ''The night is young and Lord knows when we'll ever get to your transfer stop for Virginia City. What say we eat those sandwiches and wash 'em down with some rye and tank water? A man has to keep his strength up in your company, no offense.''

As he rolled off her to fetch and carry, Natasha laughed lewdly and said, ''You *did* lay Calamity Jane, didn't you? How could she have told me how you were hung if she'd never had that glorious maypole in her?''

Longarm shrugged his bare shoulders and replied, ''I never claimed I'd never kissed any other gals around Deadwood. Mayhaps it pays to advertise, or mayhaps old Calamity just has a vivid imagination. She swears she has a daughter named Jean by Wild Bill Hickok. Old James Butler Hickok, as we really knew him, assured me personally it wasn't so. They both told lies when the truth was in their favor, but Jim usually favored good-looking gals and vice versa. So I tend to buy his claim he'd have bedded a clean young cowboy first. Calamity gave birth to her kid in Montana back around '73. Hickok was treading the boards of the wicked stage with Buffalo Bill Cody in a play they called *Scouts of the Plains* in '73. Next case.''

Natasha sat naked as a jay against the bulkhead as she nibbled her sandwich while Longarm made them drinks. When she pointed out that a gal most often started a baby nine months earlier, Longarm handed her a tepid glass of water and Maryland rye, saying, "Same difference. I don't see how the two of them could have met up before the fall of '74 when Hickok first rode for Calamity's stamping grounds, which you say you just came from. Old Calamity *was* down Kansas way around '70. I met her professionally that summer in Dodge. She wasn't that old-looking then. But whether Hickok or myself had messed with her in '70, I fail to see how she could have born either one of us a bastard three years later. Hickok was married to a way nicer-looking circus gal called Agnes Lake when he made the mistake of buying a few drinks for a local character called Calamity Jane, just before he got shot.''

Natasha sipped her drink and allowed that they were surely talking about a local character. She asked if he still thought she herself was a big fibber.

He sat bare-assed on the edge of the bunk to inhale some ham and cheese on rye before he told her, "Have it your own way. You'd be the one and original Tiger Tasha, dealing square from the box with a deck of those Tiger Brand faro cards our mothers all warned us about.''

She pouted, "All the stripes on all the tigers you'll find on the backs of *my* faro cards are exactly the same. I don't *have* to cheat. The odds of faro favor the dealer by four to fifteen percent.''

He washed some grub down and replied, "Those odds weren't enough to save Madame Mustache down Bodie way. But let's not argue how high up might extend, or what there might have been before the very beginning of time. Do you want to read the little we really have on those mysterious killings they want me to look into?''

She shook her unbound head, as if to sweep bread crumbs from her big bare tits, and said, ''Good heavens. Can't you just *tell* me why they're sending you to California if you want to get it off your chest?''

He said he'd be getting back on *her* chest as soon as he got his second wind. Then he said, ''Whether you read about it or hear about it, there ain't all that much. As you doubtless know, there's a fair-sized Chinatown in Frisco, with smaller but solidly Chinese settlements up in the Mother Lode country of the Sierra Nevadas. It ain't the *High* Sierras you prospect for color. The gold reefs that run north and south seem to favor the roots of oak and manzanita. You hardly ever strike gold further up the slopes where the sugar pine and ponderosa grows.''

She asked if he found that important.

He said, ''Yep. You don't find Chinese prospecting higher, or much farther east than Angel's Camp, where Mark Twain put that frog-jumping contest and the rough but mostly good-natured whites of the Mother Lode country tolerate Chinese more than in some other places. Panning for gold in Montana can take fifty years off an average Chinaman's life, and Leadville passed a city ordinance against a Chinese running loose within the city limits.''

She asked how many Sons of Han he'd ever seen up around Deadwood, and he had to admit, ''Not many. I follow your drift, and I said there was no sense arguing about your kissable cheekbones. My point is that you have all those Chinese in the Frisco Chinatown and all those Chinese up in the Sierra foothills, with nothing much between but stock and produce growers who ain't got much use for Chinese and ain't averse to speaking their mind. So Sons of Han having business in the hills beyond them get there by way of the Sacramento riverboats that steam from Frisco

28

across the bay and up through the delta, where the waters of the Great Valley of California come together sort of confusingly. You can lose your way and then some in such frog-infested tule and cattails. The riverboats thread slowly through a mess of natural and man-dredged channels, because they shift some as the river waters fight the tides from the west. Once you work your way through the delta, it's a faster run up to the state capital by way of a broad clear channel betwixt open range along both banks.''

She asked what that was supposed to mean, as if she didn't care.

He told her, "Passengers boarding the Sacramento riverboats seem to wind up missing, according to the folks who claim to have been waiting to meet them. Some of the men who never made it to the end of the passage they'd paid for were white. Others were Chinese. None of the missing white men have ever been seen again. A good many Chinese known to have boarded the river steamers alive and well have been fished out of the Frisco Bay or Sacramento River, once the tides and currents got tired of playing ball with 'em. The lawmen I'm headed west to help suspect all those victims must have gone over the rail after dark somewhere in the mostly uninhabited delta. I see why they suspect that. Somebody would be more likely to come forward if they'd seen a man go overboard in broad day as they were threshing a wheat field or herding cows along a river road. We're still working on how come none of the missing *white* men have bobbed up anywhere. The notion that they might have been weighed down by more gold dust than your average Chinese falls apart as soon as you consider the motive anybody would have for doing any of them in.''

She asked if he knew how the victims they'd found had been killed.

He said, "Sure. Didn't they tell you they'd all been stabbed in the back? All but that one, that is?''

29

She muttered, "Bastard. I'll get you for that. What about the one who wasn't stabbed?"

Longarm said, "Oh, he was stabbed, same as the others. But he must have been mighty tough as well as a hell of a swimmer. He stumbled into the camp of some market hunters gathering ducks in the delta. He'd been stabbed fatally before he'd swum himself to death. But they did what they could for him, and naturally asked him who'd killed him."

She asked who the dying Chinese had accused.

Longarm said, "*Them.* He told the hunter holding his hand that *he* was the one. Then he died."

She shrugged her bare shoulders and decided, "He must have been delirious. Or maybe all white men looked alike to him."

Longarm said, "That's fair. Seeing we have trouble telling *them* apart. But what do you make of the dying statement of the late Gum How, discovered in a state of disrepair on land near a Barbary Coast house of ill repute?"

She said she'd never heard of such a person, and added, "Didn't you just say all but that one victim who'd made it ashore had been dead when they hit the water?"

Longarm explained, "Gum How hadn't been tossed off a river steamer. The purser's mate saw him going ashore at the end of the downriver run. His kith and kin say they expected him to board a later boat. Somebody else must have met him on the quay. An hour or so later, a soiled dove throwing slops out a back window heard him moaning in the alley and sent for the law. Two copper badges found a dying Chinese with a stab wound in his back and nothing in his pockets. As he lay there dying, he named one of the copper badges trying to help him as his killer."

She washed down the last of her sandwich and held out the empty glass as she said, "Brrr, that does sound spooky. I've heard of crazy people killing others. But crazy people being killed en masse by who knows who or why? What if those white men who *say* they found a dying China-man—"

"Won't work," Longarm cut in, pouring water in her empty glass to cut the rye as he explained. "The hunters who found the one dying victim could have been crazy enough to say a man they'd stabbed had said they'd stabbed him. I find it harder to buy two Frisco copper badges responding to a streetwalker's complaint about a moaning man in an alley right after they'd stabbed him there. The Frisco police patrol the Barbary Coast along the docks in pairs. Chinamen ain't supposed to be there at all. So anybody could have stabbed him. But three witnesses, counting the soiled dove, distinctly heard him say one of the copper badges had done the dirty deed—about fifteen minutes earlier, to hear the medical examiner tell it."

Natasha allowed that the whole thing was a real poser, and asked if he felt up to screwing her some more.

He did. It felt grand. But then, as all things must, it ended as out of breath as before, and they lay there cuddled atop the covers to share a smoke while, out in the night, somebody tore by at full gallop and someone else yelled in the distance, "What in blue blazes could be taking that army train so long?"

Longarm passed her the cheroot, murmuring, "We ought to be on our way before midnight."

She took a deep drag, passed it back, and marveled, "My God, can it still be so early? I've seldom gotten started this way before the wee small hours and . . . I've been thinking about going on to Virginia City, Custis. I don't suppose there's any way I could get you to . . . sort of lay over with me in Nevada for a while?"

He said, "I would if I could but I can't," and that was only half a lie. For she was grand in bed and pleasant company when they had pause for breath, whether she ever told the truth or not.

He patted her soft bare shoulder and said soothingly, "This is a private compartment with a door that bolts on the inside and we have a long trip ahead of us, old pal. They'll be switching this car onto a Central Pacific engine

31

by the Great Salt Lake, and we can make love with the blinds wide open for many a wide-open mile after that.''

She said, "I've been thinking about how far it will be to come back alone once I get to Virginia City to find Madame Mustache no longer there.''

He asked what she aimed to do about that. He wasn't surprised to hear her say, "Before I heard Madame Mustache had opened a new place out Nevada way, I'd been considering Durango, that newer boomtown to the southwest of Leadville.''

Longarm allowed he'd been to Durango, found it tolerable, and a lot closer than Virginia City. So they smoked some more and screwed some more, and then Natasha went back to her own compartment—she said—to gather her own baggage while she made up her mind whether to go on with him or quit while she was ahead.

She must have decided to quit while she was ahead. She never came back while the train was stalled at Bitter Creek, or after it moved on. So he was having breakfast alone in the dining car the next morning, admiring the Great Salt Lake outside, when that railroad detective from the night before joined him for just a cup, saying he was sure glad things were back to just running late.

Longarm allowed he wasn't feeling quite so tense that morning. It was juvenile to kiss and tell, and if he hadn't learned anything by playing along with the enemy, it hadn't hurt worth mentioning.

The railroad detective broke into his train of thought by smiling slyly as he said, "I see you made out pretty well with Tiger Tasha back in Bitter Creek, you dog.''

Longarm frowned, and replied it wasn't polite to listen with your fool ear against a door panel. Then he asked if his old pal was sure the lady they were gossiping about was really called Tiger Tasha.

The railroad detective said, "Sure I'm sure. I know her of old from Omaha, and I hear she's been dealing up Deadwood way and . . . What's so funny all of a sudden?''

To which Longarm could only reply, "Me. But that's all right. I might never have moved so directly if I'd known the lady was the lady she kept *saying* she was.''

Chapter 5

The original travel orders called for Longarm to get off the train at Sacramento and catch the steamer down to the delta stop at Reedport. Then a gal who didn't look the least bit Chinese got on at Elko, and with one thing and another Longarm stayed on to the end of the line across the bay from Frisco.

The gal who got on at Elko was neither one thing nor the other. Longarm didn't ignore his original travel orders just because she was willing to let him kiss her and nothing more on the observation platform. That Indian attack had thrown off his time of arrival at the inland city of Sacramento, and he wanted to steam through that delta in the dark. So he stayed on the train when it made Sacramento early in the afternoon, and raced the day boat to the Frisco bay the long way round.

Trains ran faster than river steamers, but not on water or even mushy ground. So the tracks ran south from Sacramento for Stockton, crossing streams smaller than the Sacramento River, and continued a good ways south to cross the small San Joaquin at Lathrop and then head west again south of the ill-defined delta—roughly thirty by ten miles in area, with most of the mud contributed from the more seasonal San Joaquin as it ran up from the south and tried to crawl in bed with a wider and swifter Sacramento.

Once they'd worked west of the big marshy delta, the tracks had to swing way north around the Diablo Mountains between the Big Valley and the Frisco Bay. By the time they could swing south some more at San Pablo, you could see the upper bay out the right-hand windows. It was only a few minutes south to Oakland Town, where you could catch a ferry across the bay to Frisco—or San Francisco, as the descendants left over from old Spanish times preferred to call it.

The gal who got on at Elko was going on to Frisco. But Longarm, his baggage, and Winchester stayed in Oakland for the time being.

He wasn't sore at the gal. It was her misfortune and none of his own if she thought stopping at finger-fucking left her pure for the man who was good enough to marry up with her. That other gal with the slanty eyes and more willing ways had made him alert to the possibility that any number of others might be expecting him to come from Denver. So whether Tiger Tasha had been who she said she was or not, he'd told her he was getting off at Sacramento. He *hadn't* gotten off at Sacramento, and if he didn't land at the foot of Market Street with the other passengers off the train, he was likely to confound considerably anyone watching for him.

Having decided that, he didn't have a hell of a lot to do in the mighty sleepy town of Oakland, which had been built where it stood by natural error.

At first glance, anybody gazing down at a map of Frisco Bay could see it made more sense to build the main port on the mainland, facing west toward the Golden Gate to the wide Pacific, instead of out on that hilly peninsula where the benighted Spaniards had laid out the seaport of Yerba Buena to serve the mission of San Francisco de Assisi. It seemed a hell of a place to build a railroad terminal, and so they'd laid out the more sensibly located Oakland before it was generally agreed that those mud flats extending way out from the eastern shores of the bay made for a really piss-poor deep-water port. But what the hell, Oakland was still a handy place to end the transcontinental Pony Express, Overland Trail, Central Pacific Railroad, and such. You only had a short and pleasant ferry ride ahead of you, Lord willing and there wasn't too much of that famous Frisco fog.

Longarm checked his baggage at a cheap boardinghouse near the ferry building, wired home to Billy Vail about his new time of arrival, and ate some famous Frisco oysters from the Oakland mud flats before he took in a vaudeville show featuring a sea lion that played tunes on some horns, a gal who juggled plates in pink tights, and a young song-and-dance man Longarm had met before in Dodge. He called himself Eddie Foy. Longarm was tempted to go backstage after the show and invite the kid out for a drink. But he doubted Eddie Foy would know much about missing white men or murdered Chinese, and it was getting on toward sundown. So Longarm went back to the boarding-house for his baggage, and toted the load aboard a ferry. You could barely make out the far shore as the sun sank ruby red behind an evening fog bank.

Gents who had never been to Frisco sang songs about watching the sun go down through the Golden Gate. But you couldn't *see* the Golden Gate from the bay ferries, or stare out at the sunset through it from most parts of Frisco. Longarm had caught an outlaw in a lie about that one time. As he stood on the foredeck of the ferry with his left hand gripping the slot of his bulky McClellan, the boat was inching its way and tooting its steam siren for what seemed a million years before, at last, they crashed into the ferry slip of redwood piling and he got off before they could bounce back and sink.

He was glad about the ever-thickening fog as he asked his way to the nearby river steamer piers. There was nobody in line ahead of him in the dimly lit ticket office. A helpful older clerk set Longarm straight about the particular boat he wanted to catch if he aimed to get off at Reedport. Then he tried to talk Longarm into staying in town overnight, explaining, "I can't promise they'll shove off before this fog lifts, and if they do, I can't promise they'll ever find the way through the damned delta. You might wind up in Sacramento and have to come back downstream tomorrow. If I was you I'd check into the Palace. Or mayhaps the Seaman's Rest if you can't afford the Palace."

Longarm allowed he could sleep aboard a grounded river steamer as well as in any fool hotel. So he got his ticket, had to smoke in their waiting room for a million years, and finally got to board the damned boat.

The Sacramento riverboats were walking-beam side-paddle steamers. They looked nothing like the wedding cakes you saw on most inland rivers of the day. They were built along the same lines, if not by the same builders, as the partly oceangoing steamers of the Fall River Line that ran up and down Long Island Sound, with pointy bows, rounded-off sterns, and air-filled sponsons angled out to either side at the waterline to cope with any rough water.

The one Longarm boarded that evening was called *Miss Lola Montez* after the late belly dancer and belle of the California Gold Rush. They said that in her day the Irish spitfire with the Spanish stage name had danced with rubber tarantulas and screwed most every man of note, from the king of Bavaria to the editor of the *San Francisco Courier*, and nobody had ever accused her of being frigid.

But alas, she'd burned herself out and died in Brooklyn about the time a young Custis Long was running off to the War Between the States. But what the hell. He was never going to sleep with Nel Gwynn or Lisa Hamilton either, thanks to time's cruel teeth.

The staterooms and promenade deck were topside above the paddle box to either side, and the cargo decks were fore and aft of the central boilers and massive steam cylinders. So Longarm found the stateroom he'd paid for, mainly to avoid having to share with a stranger, and stored his heavily laden saddle on the top berth.

Then he took off his gunbelt and hung it on one bulkhead. He hadn't gone insane. A decoy that looked like a hawk would be less tempting than a decoy that could pass for a duck. So he dug through one saddle bag for the snub-nosed Webley .445 Bulldog he'd packed for this very occasion, and tucked it in the right side-pocket of his loosely hung frock coat before he stepped out on the dark deserted promenade and locked up, inserting a match stem in the crack below a bottom hinge to warn him on his return about uninvited guests.

The boat was still moored to the pier in the fog as Longarm moved aft along the port rail with a fuzzy bird's-eye view of the dimly lit gangplank and the damp wood-block pavement of the empty pier. The aft salon was well lit, and when he paused by one glazed door to glance in, he saw two card games were already in progress, with a thin scattering of more wary travelers bellied up to the bar.

He doubted anybody out to stab him and throw him overboard would be lurking in the lamplit after-salon. So he drifted on, eyes darting discreetly under the pulled-down brim of his pancaked coffee Stetson.

He circled the whole blamed boat without meeting up with another soul on deck. So he moved down an outside stairway—sailors would call it a ladder, but it still looked like a stairway—and saw that, sure enough, some lesser lights were shooting craps on the open forward deck ahead of the cargo space.

You paid about the same for first- or second-class passage aboard the train or boat up to Sacramento, and depending on the timetables, either could get you there first. But the train charged extra for any baggage too heavy to tote, having much less room in the baggage car up forward. So serious mining men, merchants, and sly dogs who wanted to share a romantic cruise in a more spacious private stateroom with the lady of their choice took the steamboat up the slower but shorter river route to Sacramento. At six or eight knots, depending on the currents, the steamer would get them there come morning, Lord willing and it ever cast off in this infernal fog.

Longarm didn't join the crap game. He knew anybody preying on the roughly dressed whites or blue-pajama'd Chinese gathered around the galloping dominoes would be choosing victims from the far edges of the gathering. Sure enough, as Longarm casually glanced around, he spied another cuss in a dark suit and high-heeled boots under a foursquare Stetson, holding up a cargo crib with his own back as he gazed in idle curiosity at everything in sight.

Longarm knew the dark stranger had noticed him as well when the much smaller figure detached itself from the slats of the crib to head his way.

Longarm hadn't buttoned the front of his own coat to begin with. He tried not to tense up visibly as the small dark dapper cuss came silent as a tabby cat despite his cowboy boots. Then the tension was broken as a pleasant girlish voice called out, "Longarm! What are you doing aboard this tub at this hour, you old basser?"

Longarm had met the young squirt before, on about as friendly terms as it was possible to meet a youth who'd have made Billy the Kid shit his pants.

Longarm said, "Howdy. We were just talking about you when I was coming out from Cheyenne. I've been studying on how I might look you up. Nobody in Chinatown will allow they've ever heard of you when one of us round-eyed devils asks, Pete."

The small Oriental, dressed like a dapper white stockman, hissed, "No *names*, damn it! Let's talk up on the promenade deck!"

Longarm turned toward the steps, but complained, "You just called out *my* name, didn't you?"

His small admirer replied, "Shit, everybody knows you long-nosed lawmen are after the river pirates who keep knocking off paid-up members of all six tongs. I'm working in secret for the Hip Sings and Suey Ongs. I think I told you the last time we met what the Hip Sings and Suey Ongs think of one another. So that's how hot this bullshit has become in Chinatown!''

By this time they were topside and Longarm had a better look at the deadly squirt as they passed a lit-up stateroom window.

Fung Jin Toy, or Little Pete as he was better known to the San Francisco police, looked about fourteen, but had to be somewhere in his late teens or early twenties. Born somewhere, sometime, in China, Little Pete had been raised, or raised himself, on the dangerous streets of Frisco between Grant Avenue and the Barbary Coast, east of the more proper slopes of Nob and Russian Hills. Speaking English with the clean-cut accent the West Coast was starting to grow, he'd felt free to socialize and do business with either the Chinese or Barbary Coast communities. Older gents of either persuasion who found Fung Jin Toy too young or uncouth for their hand of friendship had a way of not getting any older. For Little Pete was a man of his word to his pals, and a dedicated enemy to anyone who crossed him. So whether he was old enough to vote yet or not, the harmless-looking little shit had lost track of the women he'd owned or the men he'd killed or ordered killed. In recent years the traditional old-country tongs had commenced to back more respectable enterprises such as chop suey joints, laundries, and the Chinese Lottery, or to help with the passage of an honorable picture bride from far-off Canton to America, or the Golden Mountain. The tong undertakers would ship your Chinese bones home for proper burial among your own ancestors, and if you needed some good smoking opium, the tongs could get it for you far cheaper than you could buy it in any Frisco drugstore. But they left most of the rougher opium dens and bodacious back-alley whorehouses to highbinders such as Little Pete, who was said to put his male and female sex slaves to work in a sweatshop as soon as they got too old or too clapped-up to offer the delights of forbidden fruit at a price any Chinamen would pay.

Pausing in a pool of foggy shadow to offer the young highbinder a cheroot and light one for himself, Longarm said, "I'm just as glad to hear hatchet men are hunting our mysterious river pirates, instead of the other way around. What can you tell your dear old Uncle Sam about his own nephews vanishing into thin air along this line, Pete?"

The hatchet man held the cheroot without puffing on it as he said, "If I could tell you shit we wouldn't be having this dumb conversation. The cocksuckers who've been stabbing our boys would be sleeping with the fishes, without their balls attached to them. We don't give a shit about *your* boys. When *our* boys come back down from the Mother Lode they usually bring tribute to their tongs, if you see what I mean."

Longarm said, "I see what you mean, Pete. Ain't you going to smoke that cheroot? They cost me a nickel for three."

The truly dreadful little Chinaman shook his head and held the lit but barely tasted cheroot out to Longarm, saying, "I don't smoke. I don't chew. I don't get sucked by girls who do."

To which Longarm could only reply with a sincere laugh, "It's good to hear there's *some* bad habits you don't seem to have. I'll keep my eye on the whites aboard this tub. You keep watching those cargo-deck Chinese, and if you spot anything, come get me and we'll try to take him alive. Nobody talks worth mentioning when you cut off their balls and drown 'em."

Chapter 6

They cast off at last to foghorn north dead slow, until they'd left the North Beach and Pelican or Alcatraz Island off their port stern. Then, as if they'd forged on through a swamping glass wall, they were out of the fog and picking up speed in the upper reaches of Frisco Bay under a clear starry sky.

The smaller San Pablo Bay stuck out like a big calabash pipe aimed inland from the head of the bigger bay. As *Miss Lola Montez* swung her sharp bows that way, a full moon was rising between the dark hills to either side, lighting a patch across smooth open water ahead as the pilot tooted a higher and happier note and called for full steam ahead.

Longarm was joined by other first-class passengers in the bows as they steamed east in the moonlight. Nobody seemed out to attack him, and a couple were right pretty. But when they commenced to sing about Sweet Betsy from Pike together, Longarm drifted aft toward gloomier parts.

He didn't meet up with anybody, gloomy or otherwise, until after they'd stopped at Port Costa in the narrows to pick up more cargo and passengers, when they were navigating the ever-widening waters of the inland bay. But Little Pete rejoined him in the stern on the upper deck as clumps of salt rush commenced to sprout from the moonlit surface to both sides of the main channel. They were passing a bell buoy when the young highbinder told him they were entering the delta. Longarm said he never would have guessed.

The side paddles up forward were taking more delicate bites at the surface now. Nobody wanted to run aground at night in a tricky channel. Longarm quietly observed he'd thought Little Pete was keeping an eye on those Sons of Han down on the cargo deck.

Little Pete said, "I am. Did you think I'd be dumb enough to come aboard alone?"

Longarm allowed he hadn't noticed any other likely hatchet men, and Little Pete said, "You're not supposed to. Anyone who tries to stab or chop me is in for lots of surprises. But to tell the truth, we're not expecting trouble heading inland. All of our boys who've been hit were headed west from the gold fields."

"With how much gold?" asked Longarm.

The Oriental said, "We don't know. None of the victims were found with any gold on them. But none of them went up in the Mother Lode country to pick mushrooms. The last time I tried to tell you how tough it could be for a Chinese in your country, you suggested I go back to *my* country."

"I never meant that as insulting, old son," Longarm said. "It's a plain fact that us born Americans get tired of hearing folks who busted a gut getting here complain about how awful it is. I'd be lying if I said Miss Columbia was pure of sin and never showed her bitchy side. But like I told you that other time, if I found myself in China and just couldn't stand the place, I'd get on the first boat headed back to my native shores."

Fung Jin Toy smiled like the mean little kid he was and replied, "Shit, you can make more money in your country by accident than you could ever make in my country on purpose. The point I was trying to make was that our boys can't dig for riches in the Golden Mountain anywhere they

43

want to. Your boys can be moody. Sometimes we can get along with you and sometimes we can't. So you don't find Chinese in all the gold camps up in the Sierra Nevadas. The bearded pink devils of Nevada County are inclined to hang Ching Chong Chinaman by his pigtail, while the easier-going miners of Calaveras County would as soon amuse themselves with frog-jumping contests.''

Longarm said, ''So I've heard. Did Mark Twain write that story about a real Murphy's Camp tradition, or was it the other way around?''

Little Pete shrugged and said, ''I wasn't there. I only know they bet big money on those red-legged frogs every summer, and they allow our boys to bet. They won't hire Chinese as drillers or loaders over in those deep-shaft Hearst diggings near Murphy's Camp. But they don't care who pans for color along the creeks as long as it's not upstream of any round-eyed sourdoughs. So a Son of Han who minds his manners and pans from dawn to dusk can still make more than any white boss is about to pay him. Nobody would be dumb enough to pile up more than a few hundred dollars worth of gold dust before he brought it down from the hills for his tong to bank for him. So we're not talking about that mythical Chinese who drowned at sea when he wouldn't let go of his heavy gold pokes. We're talking about no more than a pound or so in a handy package. Stab. Grab. Away we go! We're hoping to spot the sons of bitches as they're headed back upstream. They'd hardly be on the alert for a gold panner on his way to pan for gold, see?''

Longarm asked who they might suspect. The soft-spoken but hard-eyed highbinder said, ''You long-nosed lawmen talk silly. If we suspected anybody they wouldn't be around to suspect. We don't have to fuck with your rules of evidence.''

Longarm had no call to warn a hatchet man for hire that vigilante justice could lead to the guilty going free as the innocent died. He asked what Little Pete could tell him

44

about Tiger Tasha. He wound up telling Little Pete about the exotic gal who claimed to be guilty of dealing with those notorious Tiger Brand faro cards.

Longarm knew Little Pete had been known to fib to the law. But he sounded sincere as he replied, "None of the Frisco tong's work. Nobody sends *bu how day* out to kill one another by mistake. I'd have been told if such a woman was working for the people *I'm* working for."

Longarm grimaced and said, "You sound like a railroad dick I know. She couldn't have been pure Chinese. Some of the men missing off those riverboats were even whiter. How do you feel about a mixed bunch of both breeds preying on anybody down from the hills with considerable funds in compact form?"

Then he asked, "What can you tell us about that Chinese found dying along the Barbary Coast? The one who accused the copper badges that a lady of the evening had summoned of being the ones who stabbed him earlier."

Little Pete replied, "We heard about that. He belonged to the Yun Ying tong. He'd just come down from the hills, but nobody but the Yun Yings know if he had anything on him. So it doesn't mean anything one way or the other when the Yun Yings say he hadn't reported in to them yet. Those beat coppers probably heard him wrong. You boys repeat what our boys say sort of crazy."

Longarm insisted, "I've read the transcript. Two lawmen and a whore agree on the dying man's last words and they don't sound crazy. He said, and I quote, 'I knew you gonna killy poor me. You belly bad joss. Goddamy you!' "

Little Pete shrugged and said, "Joss can mean prayer or luck. Maybe he was talking about the whore who says she found him. Maybe he was out to change his luck with white meat and her pimp stabbed him and lifted his poke."

Longarm said, "That works for the Barbary Coast. What about those duck shooters who found a dying Chinese in the reeds, asked him who'd done it, and agreed he said, and again I quote exactly, 'It was you did this to me. I

45

should have listened. They told me you would be the end of me!' ''

Longarm stared soberly out at the inky marshland they were threading their way through, with the moonlight bright on open water, as he went on. "That transcript reads as better English. The poor cuss must have spent more time around my kind. But whether we all look alike to your kind or not, I don't see how those hunters could have stabbed, grabbed, and then pretended to be helping a man other witnesses distinctly saw boarding a river steamer way the hell upstream!"

Little Pete grumbled, "We still think the killers have to be white men. You *do* look alike to us, and more than that, there are so damned *many* of you next to our boys."

Longarm smiled thinly and said, "I heard there were more folks who ate with chopsticks than you could shake a chopstick at if they'd all hold still to be counted."

Little Pete shrugged modestly and said, "Not on this side of the ocean. We're what you call a downtrodden minority, and the few like me who can almost pass for native sons are rare as diamonds. When you just can't spot a likely suspect, it's smart to suspect somebody less obvious. So we suspect some round-eyed cocksuckers are killing and robbing our boys of their hard-earned gold, and when we catch up with them . . ."

"You told me about their balls," Longarm said. "How come you keep saying *they,* plural? Ain't it possible we're up against some solitary monster such as Cannibal Packer or Liver Eating Johnston?"

The monstrous young highbinder said, "You don't pan gold from dawn to dusk if you're a weakling, and the tongs have put out the word to be watching out for back-stabbing thieves. The only way you're going to take out a strong and sober gold panner calls for two or three on one. One to grab and one to stab, see?"

Longarm pursed his lips thoughtfully and gazed at a far-off pinpoint of light as he replied, "You'd expect them to be stabbed in the aorta from the front if they were first grabbed from behind. Might there be any Chinese folks hunting or dwelling out here in the middle of this mighty big marsh, Pete?''

The highbinder nodded, but said, ''Hunting and fishing. Not dwelling. There's crabs, oysters, and prawns for the taking if you poke around in the side channels. Nobody but a total asshole would want to *live* in that muggy green hell. I've heard there are some white trash living on rafts up and down the river. Assholes, as I just said. None of my own people spend more time than they have to over this way. That lamplight you've been admiring probably goes with some tar-paper shack on a sugar-pine raft. Are you expecting them to board us with knives gripped in their teeth?''

Longarm allowed he wasn't, and headed forward again as the whistle above commenced to signal a landing ahead. He went to his own stateroom, found the match stem on the deck, but assumed it had been Little Pete when he found nobody laying for him and nothing missing.

He toted his load down to the cargo deck, where he found a young couple with their own baggage by the gangway gate.

When he asked, they told him they were indeed coming up on Reedport, over an hour late. He didn't care. It didn't hurt to get there late when you were disbarking early from an overnight run.

He asked them if there was a hotel in the river port ahead. They seemed to think that was awfully funny. The husband explained Reedport was little more than a landing at the end of some rare dry land running out through the delta marshland to the open channel. His wife invited Longarm to stay with them at their cattle spread until he could get settled in. But when it turned out they raised cows and kids a six-hour ride to the north, he had to decline their gracious offer. He told them he'd been invited to Reedport by the law there, and they agreed it was up to Marshal

Seaforth to find him and his saddle a place to stay.

You could hardly tell when they pulled in to the one pier at Reedport. There were no street lamps. A few windows back from the water were lit by lamps. Other than that, it was a good thing the moon was shining full.

Nobody was there to meet any passengers. The young couple knew their way home, and wished Longarm luck as they left him standing on the pier with his load. But there were a handful of dock workers unloading some cargo. So Longarm asked for directions, and had no trouble finding the house they said Marshal Seaforth used as his head-quarters when he was in Reedport.

The place came with a picket fence and a dog that barked as if it was being tortured by Comanche women. A gal in a light gingham dress came out to shut the yard dog up, and Longarm was able to ask her help in tracking down Tavish Seaforth.

She yelled back that she was kin to the older lawman and invited him in, adding that they'd about given him up for lost if he was the Chinese expert from Colorado.

As he opened the gate to brave the growling yard dog, he assured her he was neither Chinese nor all that expert, but confessed, "I did come out this way from Colorado. It wasn't easy. Indian trouble along the U.P. right-of-way."

He left his load on the porch and followed her inside, where the lamplight gave him a better look at her. He caught her name as Mary, and she was a handsome gal if you liked them long and lean with copper-colored hair braids framing a freckled face.

She allowed she was Marshal Seaforth's niece by mar-riage. Longarm had already noticed her infernal wedding ring. She led him back to her kitchen and sat him at a deal table, saying, "You've my leave to smoke if you want. I'll put the coffee on while we wait for Uncle Tavish. I just can't say when he'll be back. He and some deputies had to go up to Rio Vista on some emergency."

He asked how long a ride they were talking about, and

she told him they didn't patrol the delta much on horseback. As she bent over and poked the banked fire in her kitchen range awake, Longarm regretted that wedding ring even more. There was more to her behind than her gingham skirts and apron gave away at first.

She stood back up to explain that the marshal had his own steam launch to take him where neither a rider nor riverboat could go in the tidal channels of the sprawling delta.

She said the small but powerful launch got around the delta fast. They'd barely finished their scones and coffee when he saw she was right. That yard dog was yapping again and she brightened, saying, "That must be Uncle Tavish now!"

Longarm followed her out front to hush the dog and greet a taller and leaner version of Billy Vail.

As they shook, Longarm said he was sorry he'd shown up late. The older lawman sounded less crusty than Billy Vail as he said, "Better late than never. You couldn't have been aboard the steamer that poor cuss boarded at least a week ago."

Longarm agreed that sounded convincing, and asked who they might be talking about.

Marshal Seaforth replied, "Another Chinaman, last seen coming out of the mountains after eight weeks of panning for color. My deputies have hauled him over to the icehouse to pack him proper for shipping on to his next of kin. I hate it when they've been in the water that long before they're found. Some Mex kids spotted this last one bobbing in the shallows up near Rio Vista. Lord knows how far his poor bloated carcass drifted from where he was knifed and shoved overboard."

Chapter 7

You didn't get too tired riding in a boat. So it only took two scones and a cup of coffee to get Marshal Seaforth to invite Longarm for a look at the latest victim. His niece wanted to tag along, but they wouldn't let her. She stamped a foot and said she'd seen dead folks aplenty in her time. But Marshal Seaforth shook his head and said, "Not *this* dead, *mo caileag*. Freshly packaged for a funeral is one thing. Bloated to bursting is another, and we'll say no more about it."

Longarm didn't want to brag about Shiloh, so he just nodded at her with a sorry smile and followed the older lawman outside. He saw they were retracing the way he'd just come from the river landing. He'd noticed the big ice-house near the pier in passing. Like most transshipping points of the era, Reedport sold fresh-made ice to replace what had melted around produce on its way to market. Old Seaforth hadn't told his deputies to haul rotting meat into the main plant where well water was frozen in copper molds by circulating ammonia from the steam compresser out back. They'd put the body under a coal-oil lamp on the loading dock, crated on a bed of crushed ice and rock salt.

As anyone who'd ever cranked ice cream knew, salting ice got it colder than its regular freezing point. But the

50

horror in the wet crate still reeked of death to high heaven.

When you killed a gent and left him unembalmed in warm weather, he got waxy pale where he didn't turn puce lower down. Then, as he digested himself for a spell, his lower belly turned purple, green, or both, and commenced to swell, then swell some more, as the rest of him bloated and discolored till he looked like a fat man who'd been boiled in a lobster pot. A corpse bloated sooner and much worse underwater. So the dead Chinese they'd found in the shallows had split the seams of his blue denim pajamas, and his face looked more like a Halloween jack-o'-lantern than anything that had ever smiled at a kid or admired a pretty ankle.

Longarm told the senior lawman in charge, "I'll take your word you were able to identify him officially because nobody else he could be has been reported missing after booking passage to Frisco in Sacramento. But I wish a Chinaman who just said we all look the same could see this poor specimen. I know this sounds disgusting, but sometimes you can get a better likeness to the way a man was in life if you let him rot a tad more."

One of the younger deputies suddenly ran off into the dark. The marshal grimaced and said, "Don't teach an old dog new tricks. Billy Vail told me you served in the war. So did I. I noticed at Malvern Hill how the battlefield dead who hadn't been buried or eaten by pigs by the time they'd turned black had started to look skinny again. But if we hold this one too long, we'll wind up stuck for the cost of his burial when his kith and kin lose interest."

Longarm shook his head and said, "They won't lose interest. If he hadn't been paying tribute to one of the tongs, he wouldn't have been allowed to prospect for color among others who do. The tongs ask a lot when you consider how hard most members have to work for their money. But they do watch out for their own. They'll never let us bury a paid-up tong member in what they consider alien soil. I have it from the horse's mouth that they'll be out to avenge this old boy along with the other Sons of Han. The same horse told me any missing white men are on their own. So let's talk about *them*.''

Marshal Seaforth wanted the name of that horse, and it wasn't as if they were on opposing sides. So Longarm told him tersely about meeting up with Little Pete aboard the night boat, and repeated his own question about white men down from the Mother Lode and just plain missing.

Seaforth said, ''I told Billy Vail when I asked for you that I was turned around total in this puzzle-maze! We just don't *know* what's happened to all the white victims and some of the Chinese. You're the expert on all this Ching Chong bullshit. Suppose you tell *us* why a Chinese corpse floats better than a white one.''

The kid deputy who hadn't run off to puke chimed in to opine that white men wore heavier boots and more duds to waterlog, with more pockets full and so on.

Marshal Seaforth shot him a withering look, but sweetly demanded where the child had been when they were dragging the main fucking channel and hauling up everything from old bedsprings to long-dead livestock.

The kid shot Longarm a grateful look when Longarm pursed his lips and calmly observed, ''There's many another channel in a thirty-by-ten-mile tidal marsh, with the ocean tides and the competing river currents running the water both ways in most of 'em. How long would it take to dredge just the main side channels, Marshal?''

Seaforth shook his head and said, ''Forget it. We could die of old age before we had the delta to the south properly *mapped*. It's been tried, by the Army Engineers. They gave up after they noticed how the channels shift with little or no local warning. You get high water or low in many a mountain stream draining the Sierra Madre for hundreds of miles north or south, with the coast ranges west of the big valley likely to flood north or south whilst the sun is shining here in the delta.''

Longarm hadn't asked for an infernal geography lesson.

52

So he said he'd take the marshal's word it wasn't practical to drag for sunken corpses very far off the main channel the steamers followed through the delta. So the older man told his deputy to cover the corpse they had with more ice and rock salt for now.

Turning to Longarm, Marshal Seaforth suggested they go on back to the house for some more coffee and a sit-down discussion of the blamed case.

So Longarm headed back to what was really the home of the marshal's niece by marriage, as it turned out. Seaforth told him along the way how he'd been looking after the child after his nephew had drowned up the river a piece.

Longarm said he was sorry to hear Miss Mary was a widow woman, and asked if her late husband had been a steamboat man.

Seaforth shook his head and said, "He was driving beef across this delta slough that had never been deep enough to worry about. There'd been a wet spell over in the coast ranges and the next thing he knew, poor Duncan had ridden into quicksand. The riders with him said he'd have saved himself if he hadn't tried to save his palomino. But our Duncan *brath* could be stubborn, and he ignored the shouts of the others and drowned himself *air sgath an t'each*!"

Longarm knew Billy Vail's name was Scotch when you got him to admit it. So it wasn't surprising to hear the Gaelic coming out of an old pal of a Vail. But he still felt like asking how come neither Marshal Seaforth nor his freckled niece had any brogue to go with their grasp of the lingo.

Seaforth snorted in disgust and said, "Don't go by what Sir Walter Scott and Bobby Burns wrote about the Highlands. All that *moonlicht bra bricht nicht tonicht* bullshit was *Lowland* brogue. Until the Highland Clearances a few short years ago, hardly any Highlander spoke *any* kind of English unless he'd studied it as a foreign tongue and learned to speak it like an educated Englishman."

They strode on a few thoughtful paces, and Seaforth

added in a bitter tone, "Don't get me started on the Highland Clearances! My parents brought me West as an infant after they'd been evicted from their croft to make room for more profitable *sheep*! Men like my poor *athair* had fought and died for chiefs whose dainty sons and heirs paid them back by treating them like shit. My parents never got over all that clan loyalty bullshit, and I never knew anybody spoke English in this country until they sent me to school. But I learned fast, and you can read books in this country they don't want you to read back in Scotland the Brave. They're still moaning about a golden age that never was and reciting poems by Robbie Burns, who didn't know how to spell Highland Mary, for Chrissake!"

Longarm allowed he'd read that poem and found it tolerable. He asked what was wrong with it and Seaforth said, "To begin with, Mary, spelled his way, is an *English* name. A Highland lass with that name would spell it M-A-I-R-I, like my niece up ahead."

Longarm frowned uncertainly and said, "I thought she was telling me her name was Mary when first we met. How do you pronounce the name if you spell it Highland style?"

Seaforth said, "The same as you say Mary in the Lowlands. My point is that Burns should have known how you spell in the Highlands if he wanted to drone on and on about Maxwelton's braes being so bonnie, for Gawd's sake!"

Longarm wondered why he wondered how Scotchmen dead or alive might spell a gal's name. Then they got in the house, and he wondered more when Mary or Mairi Seaforth served them more coffee and then led the way into her parlor so she could sit at her spinet and play some old Scotch songs at them.

She never sang about Annie Laurie or Peggy Gordon in the brogue a good many regular Americans put on to sing Scotch songs, and there was nothing unusual about a well-brought-up young lady entertaining a guest with some clean songs. Her uncle by marriage had learned his own English earlier, from other kids of the forty-niners. Mairi sang in that odd new West Coast accent that Longarm had noticed Little Pete had grown up speaking.

That was it. He didn't know what it meant. But it sure beat all how a back-alley hatchet man for hire and a respectable young widow of another race entirely could sound so much alike without even trying.

Like many self-educated men, Longarm read more than he let on. So he knew Englishmen and Americans talked differently because the early settlers had come from different parts of England to hammer regional English accents into newer American regional accents, with folks from Dixie winding up different from New Englanders while neither of them spoke the King's English.

So now it had happened all over again as Americans from all parts of the country and all walks of life had joined the big gold rush a full generation back to raise West Coast kids who didn't talk like anybody else. If Mairi pronounced English words differently, it was because, having no set rules to go by, she tended to pronounce words without any peculiar sounds. She pronounced all her vowels the way an opera singer might sing them, and didn't leave out any of the letters she'd ever heard others pronounce. The new way of talking was so uniform, no one could say where a Californian stood on the social totem pole. In other parts, rich folks put on airs and tried to sound like English lords and ladies or they busted a gut trying *not* to put on airs and talked rougher than they'd ever talked when they were poor. But provided they'd both grown up west of the Sierra Nevada in the years since the gold rush, a society gal from Frisco's Nob Hill and her chambermaid talked the same way, as likely did the Frisco boy delivering groceries or a Chinese hatchet man for hire! It was a hell of a way for lawabiding folks and crooks to talk. But what in blue blazes did it mean? Why was it bothering him?

He knew Marshal Seaforth would ask the same questions if he accused anybody there of talking funny. So he just sat and listened until Mairi paused long enough for her Uncle Tavish to tell her they had to talk about dead Chinamen. She excused herself to go upstairs and from the sounds of it, beat some rugs or have a pillow fight with herself.

Longarm repeated his suggestion that they let the latest victim dry out and deflate some so they could take his picture or even a plaster cast of his face, explaining, "Dead folks ain't always who we think they are. No offense, but I see by the onionskins on the case I've read so far that other dead Chinese have already been shipped back home to Far Cathay without anyone identifying the remains for certain."

The older lawman protested, "The hell you say! Chinese kith and kin who've reported 'em missing have come forward to claim them when they were found! Before you ask me how we knew what the missing men looked like, we *couldn't* know what anybody looked like before somebody asked us to look for them, could we?"

Longarm smiled thinly and said, "Of course not. But don't you see, that leaves us having to rely on the word of paid-up tong members who've been known to fib about such details as the Chinese Lottery or just how Miss Su Ki Dik arrived in the Golden Mountain. So what if the Chinese we've been putting down on paper as murder victims were never murdered at all?"

Seaforth blinked owlishly at Longarm and said, "They were right about you. You just hate simple answers. So answer me who in hell we have packed in ice over on that loading dock if he ain't a Chinese they reported missing over a week ago."

Longarm said, "Oh, he looks Chinese to me too. That ain't saying he has to be the Chinese who came down from the hills with all that gold dust. What if he's some other Chinese, a poor one too unimportant to belong to any tong?"

Seaforth shook his head and insisted, "It's their infernal

56

tongs who've been claiming their bodies and shipping them home to China!''

Longarm nodded and said, ''I told you Little Pete, also known as Fung Jin Toy, confirmed all that this very evening. But try her *this* way. Say you're a hardworking or a thieving Chinese up in the Mother Lode country and you've come by a handsome amount of gold dust. Say you've been paying a handsome percentage of such portable wealth to a bunch of old geezers in Chinatown with long fingernails and fat asses whose only claim to the rewards of your honest or dishonest efforts is the simple fact that they'll send somebody like Little Pete after you if you don't keep paying. Then say that, like Little Pete himself, you've noticed a well-to-do gent of any persuasion can cut off his pigtail, dress up like a prosperous white man, and go anywhere he wants to with his own money.''

Seaforth frowned and said, ''But what if them hatchet men came after you and . . . *Och mo mala!* That would explain the white prospectors who've never made it down to Frisco Bay with *their* gold pokes! I don't think we're missing *honest* Chinamen at all. I think the crooked Sons of Han have been robbing everyone, yellow or white, and substituting bodies of simple coolies for their own!''

Longarm warned, ''Slow down! I said it was worth considering. Those two found still alive complicate my grand notion some. Whether they were who we were told they were or not, how come they both agreed they'd been knifed by white men?''

Seaforth started to say they hadn't said exactly that. Then he nodded and said, ''They must have meant white men in general instead of any *you* in particular. So wouldn't that mean . . .''

''Yep.'' Longarm sighed. ''If the killers are white men we're back where we started, and you're right about me suspecting it's not that simple.''

Chapter 8

Some of that thumping and bumping they'd heard turned out to be Mairi Seaforth's hospitality. She'd spread a bedstead in one spare room upstairs with fresh linens and a down comforter, before she'd come back down and made hot chocolate as a hint it was getting late.

Longarm was grateful for the comforter before morning. It got cold and clammy in the Sacramento Delta by morning at most any time of the year.

They had flapjacks and sausages with strong black coffee for breakfast, and Longarm got a better look around Reedport before it was time for the boat ride back to Frisco with the dead Chinese.

There was more to the settlement by daylight than met the eye in the dark. Aside from the icehouse surrounded by warehouses and stock pens, the steamer stop was served by the usual smithy, general store, saloon, and such. Longarm found the Western Union office, in a lean-to of the general store cum post office, a pleasant surprise, although he saw it had to be there as soon as he studied on how Marshal Seaforth had heard tell of a dead body recovered a fair piece upstream.

Longarm took advantage of the facility to wire a progress report to Billy Vail in Denver. He reversed the charges and

58

sent it by day-letter rates. It wasn't a long report because he had no call to report progress with Tiger Tasha, beyond asking for Henry to check her out in their files. But he knew Billy Vail hated to pay the nickel a word Western Union charged for straight telegrams unless the news was urgent, and in point of fact the news that they'd found another victim of the person or persons unknown wasn't going to inspire old Billy to say more than, "Get off your ass and scout for sign!"

That was what Longarm had in mind as he headed back to the pier to see if they were ready to shove off. As he passed that saloon, he noticed a burly-looking galoot dressed like Buffalo Bill on a magazine cover glaring at him from a rocking chair near the bat-wing doors. The dark Vandyke beard and shoulder-length hair under a big Mexican sombrero seemed a tad out of fashion. The fringed buckskin jacket seemed all wrong for the hat as well as the Big Valley in high summer. But you had to take a brace of Navy Colts and a Bullard repeater across the lap more seriously when their owner was wearing such an unfriendly expression on his face.

Longarm didn't have time to stride over and ask the surly son of a bitch what was eating him. He just nodded, friendly, and sashayed around the icehouse to the pier, where sure enough, he saw they were loading that box full of salted ice and spoiled meat into a launch the form and length of a New Bedford whaleboat.

A vertical steam boiler with a diamond stack rose from the center of gravity amidships. Longarm saw no side paddles. So he knew the launch was propelled by a stern screw. They had the cordwood and two deputies loaded aft of the steam boiler to stoke it and man the stern tiller. The crated cadaver was being lashed down ahead of the boiler. He didn't see Marshal Seaforth. He strode over to ask about that. One of the deputies who'd just helped them move the dead man on board and hopped back on the pier allowed that the older lawman was taking a piss.

Longarm allowed he'd wait, and casually asked if anybody there knew a local character who favored Mexican sombreros, Navy Colts, and Bullard rifles.

They all smiled wearily. One said, "That would be Miwok Mason. He says he's part Indian. He's full of shit. But don't say that to his face. He's a little touched in the head and crazy-mean all over."

"How come he's running loose?" Longarm asked mildly.

Another local lawman explained, "He's got four sections under wheat, a herd of eighteen hundred or so over in the coast range under a platoon of *vaqueros,* and a Frisco law firm that's been able to get him off on self-defense more than once."

Longarm nodded with a grimace of distaste. There had been a similar rich bastard causing trouble back in New Mexico until recently. His name had been Clay Allison, and *those* high-priced lawyers had gotten him off on at least fifteen killings, two of them of lawmen, before the ornery son of a bitch had managed to run himself over with his own buckboard. It was sad but true that few local courts were above the reach of a rich bastard, and the usually drunk and always crazy Clay Allison had never been dumb enough to commit a federal offense.

Marshal Seaforth came into view in time to break Longarm's chain of thought about spoiled brats by asking whether Longarm meant to take his saddle along.

Longarm shook his head and said, "Miss Mairi said it was jake with her if I left my possibles with her for now. I've no need for a horse in Frisco. If I feel the call for more than I have on me right now aboard those Sacramento steamers, I can pick 'em up on the way upstream or down, at a regular stop."

Tavish Seaforth noted Billy Vail had said his senior deputy thought fast on his feet. As the two of them got in the steam launch, up in the bows ahead of the crated Chinese, Longarm said he meant to wire the poor man's name to

Denver as soon as they got somebody who'd known him in life to spell it out for them.

As the deputy aft at the tiller and throttle backed them out into the channel, Seaforth pointed out that they already had the name of the poor heathen, Wong Lai. But Longarm pointed out, "You got a report that a prospector called Wong Lai was missing. You ain't had anybody who knew Wong Lai identify that mess in yonder crate."

Tavish Seaforth grumbled that he was from the older school of law enforcement, where you went with the simple answers and grabbed the first likely suspect.

They were moving downstream with the ebb tide now, at a merry clip, as Longarm smiled thinly and said, "We ought to make a good team in that case. I've always liked simple answers better than complicated ones, and it's true that nine times out of ten the most logical suspect is the guilty party. But the longer I ride for the Justice Department, the more cautious I get about grabbing, lest I grab the wrong man."

He stared out across the sunlit water at the monotonous feather-topped spartina reeds sprouting right from the surface to either side. It sobered him how little of the vast delta you could really see from this low in the open water. Spartina grew taller than a man walking through it, had any man but one been able to walk on water. He knew the tule reeds and cattails further east where the water was less salty wouldn't grow that high. But it would grow high enough, and there could be so blamed *much* of it.

Getting out a couple of cheroots and handing one to the older lawman, Longarm said, "I don't want you thinking I'd make up a whopper to illustrate a point. So the time was 1864, the place was Jackson County, Missouri, and the victim was a horse trader named Bascum. John, I think. The law grabbed logical suspects called Merrick and Sharp, and the judge and jury agreed they ought to hang forthwith. So they put up a gallows overnight, grabbed the wrong men

61

from the jail, and strung up two drunks in spite of the way they kept screaming they were innocent.''

Seaforth chuckled and said, "Served 'em right for spending the night with such bad company. What did the *real* killers scream when it came *their* turn?''

Longarm said, "Nothing. Their executions had been carried out, as far as the presiding county judge could see. He was wrong, of course, but by the time his ignorance could be overturned, the red-faced lawmen who'd hung the wrong men had turned the real killers loose. Neither Merrick nor Sharp were ever seen again in those parts.''

The older lawman decided, "Ordering your last meal and spending a sleepless night in your death cell must have a concentrating effect on one's conscience. But I'd rather we catch the right ones out this way and hang them for all this work they've been putting us through.''

They steamed on a few furlongs before a big Sacramento steamer came upstream toward them, looking even bigger from where Longarm got to view it. Their helmsman swung them closer to the wall of reeds north of the channel. The pilot at the helm of the steamer tooted his steam whistle at them and churned on past them well before the big bow wave slid under them at an angle to rock them some and sway the spartina stems so a ripple of silver-green seed plumes seemed to chase the steamer up the channel at the same pace.

Longarm pointed the cheroot between his teeth at the much closer reeds, and asked how far into them a launch that size could forge away from any channel.

The marshal said, "Barely a full length of our hull if you're talking about brute strength. But we get around, off this main channel, by following smaller ones a fathom or more in width.''

He went on to explain how the professors allowed the whole delta had once been an inland rival of the Frisco Bay they were headed for. The bigger but clearer Sacramento and the more seasonal and muddy San Joaquin had poured in from the north and south a mighty long time, slowly silting the original bay to the condition it lay in now. Most of the silt had been carried from the drier foothills to the south. So a swifter-flowing Sacramento had kept the main channel scoured near the northern edges of the sea of reeds as the muddy San Joaquin built ever and ever wider reed flats to either side of its own less certain path to the sea.

Seaforth said, "Our grain and stock growers have been reclaiming a heap of land around the edges of this delta. You can't tell from here. But there's many a quarter section or more, mostly to the north of the main channel, where they've cut drainage ditches through the reeds and piled up the spoil as dikes, the way the Dutchmen do over in Holland. Let that spartina dry out, burn it off, and plow under the roots, and you get a tolerable spread of cropland. Deadflat peat soil as only needs a little ferilizer and plenty of lime or bone meal to grow most anything in this mild climate."

He blew some tobacco smoke at the green wall they were gliding along. "You have to watch where you toss a lit smoke in reclaimed peat soil, though. Come August and no rains having fell since April out this way, you can set forty acres of crop on fire, and I don't mean the crop. I mean the plowed soil under it. Or what looks to be plowed soil."

Longarm allowed that he'd heard of other parts where such so-called soil could smolder considerably when it was dry. He said an Irishman had told him they'd dug pieces of peat from boggy patches and burned them in their fireplaces after they'd dried out.

They both agreed that that didn't seem as outlandish as the thriving industry of cow-chip gathering on the shortgrass prairies east of the Rockies.

Longarm asked if that outlandishly costumed Miwok Mason he'd seen in town grew the wheat he bragged about on reclaimed delta land.

Seaforth made a wry face and said, "I've asked him to stay on dry land, where he belongs. Him and his lawyer

63

agree it ain't a federal offense to ride out along a public wagon trace through the reeds to a steamboat landing if he wants to. I can tell by the way you said his name you share the general opinion of the asshole in these parts.''

Longarm shrugged and replied, ''I don't mind assholes that dress up for a Wild West show. There's at least three such assholes up around Deadwood, claiming to be the Deadwood Dick in those stories made up by a writer called Wheeler for *Beadle's Boy's Library*. But none of Deadwood's dicks ever glared at me armed with two six-guns and a repeating rifle!''

The older lawman nodded soberly and said, ''I've warned Miwok he's going to get his fool self killed for a lost cause. But will he listen?''

Longarm replied, ''Mayhaps he's too stuck on himself to listen. What's the lost cause he's enlisted his fool self in?''

Seaforth said, ''She served you flapjacks just this morning and you allowed they tasted swell. Miwok Mason's asked Mairi to marry up with him, or at least let him carry her to church once a week. But she won't have a thing to do with him, and he's the only one who can't see why.''

Longarm sighed and said, ''Poor bastard must be half blind. But why would he glare like that at someone he don't even know?''

Seaforth answered simply, ''He knows you. Knows you spent the night under the roof of his chosen bride-to-be. So watch your step around old Miwok if you find yourself in Reedport without me and my boys. He has his *own* boys to back his play if he takes it into his head that you've been getting anywhere with Mairi.''

Longarm snorted in disbelief and said, ''Jesus H. Christ, I was never sent all the way out here to make a play for your niece, no offense.''

Marshal Seaforth nodded soberly and said, ''None taken, and it's a good thing for all concerned. For if you *did* make a play for Mairi, I fear that, knowing your rep with the ladies, I'd have to glare some at you my ownself!''

Chapter 9

They met many another vessel large and small coming east at them, but nothing slower than the big Sacramento steamers could have overtaken them or stayed out ahead for long. Marshal Seaforth said he'd already considered river pirates steaming alongside a passenger boat in progress, but it just wouldn't work. The relative speeds weren't the problem. Nobody aboard the Sacramento steamers noticing, by day or by night, *was*. Aside from portholes facing in every direction, there were lookouts posted fore and aft to watch for anything worth worrying about. When Longarm mentioned the famous Frisco fogs, the older lawman shook his head and replied, "Not this far from the Golden Gate. Do you stand atop Telegraph Hill in Frisco, you can watch them fogs come into the harbor like spilled beer foam. They barely fill the big bowl of hills around the bay. We do get ground fog of our own further inland, but it's not as thick, and hardly ever in warm weather."

They were out on San Pablo Bay by then, a body of water that only seemed smaller than Frisco Bay on the map. Steaming against the chop in a launch that low to the water made Longarm wish it was way smaller. The salty slush in that big crate behind them was swishing back and forth as their bow and stern played seesaw, and their smokestack got to leaving a corkscrew trail of smoke against the cloudless sky.

Longarm said, "What if somebody moved in under cover of the fog a tad closer to the end of the line? That one Chinese was found on dry land after somebody stabbed and robbed him, you know."

Marshal Seaforth looked disgusted and said, "Thanks for telling me. I never read them police reports before I sent them on to Denver. The other victims found were found back yonder in the delta, and before you ask, the tides don't push much that far upstream after they spend so much force pushing through the narrows ahead and spreading out here in San Pablo Bay. The killer or killers has to be attacking them gents of Christian or heathen persuasion late at night on the night boats. And yes, we seem to be missing white and Chinese, traveling on deck and in staterooms. Nobody has the run of the whole vessel after dark. So do we suspect the whole steamship line of covering up for the killers?"

Longarm agreed that hardly seemed likely, and added, "You read about such master criminal plots in Ned Buntline's magazines. I've never yet caught a whole railroad or steamboat company robbing its own passengers and tossing them overboard. To begin with, it would be bad for business, and after that, the number of co-conspirators would make it unprofitable for all concerned as soon as it came time to split the proceeds. Not a one of those dead or missing prospectors could have been headed back to Frisco with more than a hundred pounds of gold dust, and each such stab and grab adds up to a hanging offense you wouldn't want too many pals to know about."

Seaforth nodded and said, "A dozen would be too much. Even if Frank and Jesse had pulled off that Northfield raid, there was barely enough in the First National Bank to pay for the risk once they'd split it eight ways. The most they ever made for laying their lives on the line was five thousand for each to keep and cherish, and that was the time Frank and Jesse hit the Kansas Fair cashier for ten thousand without the Younger brothers or anybody else tagging along for a cut.''

Longarm agreed that a prospector down from the hills with ten thousand on him would be a rare opportunity, and then they talked some more in circles, put in at Port Costa for some coffee and a leg stretch, and went on to make the Frisco Embarcadero by mid-afternoon. They put in at the foot of Washington Street, handy to Chinatown up the slope, to be met by the mixed delegation Marshal Seaforth had wired ahead to.

The machine that ran the city by the bay didn't hold with having heathen Chinese or even North Beach Italians on its police force. But a few wiser precinct captains had noticed the edge that policy gave over half the street gangs north of Market Street, and they'd had a few of the boyos culti-vate Cantonese or Sicilian informers and ''concerned citi-zens'' to act as go-betweens. So there were a half-dozen Orientals, dressed both Chinese and American, among the motley crew of white copper badges, detectives, and civic officials who'd come to meet the bloated corpse.

Two Chinese, one in a skullcap with a half-shaved head and pigtail, the other dressed like a regular undertaker, had lesser lights haul the heavy crate up on the pier and pry the lid open to stink the day up for yards around. The dignified old gent with the pigtail gravely identified the chilled horror in the box as a member of his own *chia* or clan, the name of which escaped him at the moment. Tong officials never admitted to belonging to a particular tong, or even *chia,* to anybody who didn't speak their particular Chinese dialect.

None of the Frisco lawmen really cared. Whoever the son of a bitch was, it seemed unlikely he'd been killed within their jurisdiction, and if the Chinese wanted to claim him they were more than welcome to him.

Marshal Seaforth had long since told Longarm he meant to wine and dine in Frisco and head back for the county seat further inland, not Reedport, unless Longarm wanted to be dropped off there to pick up his saddle and such at

Mairi's place. A man who patrolled all those reeds in a steam launch got to hang his hat in lots of places. It wouldn't have been polite to ask old Tavish how many ladies, other than that one niece by marriage, might be willing to put him up from time to time.

They'd brought a hearse down from Chinatown, but hadn't begun to shut the damned box and haul the dead man away. Longarm got out his pocket watch, saw it agreed pretty well with the lengthening shadows along the Embarcadero, and started to edge away from the chatty crowd.

Marshal Seaforth caught up, asking him where he was headed. Longarm said, "Back to work. I'll wire you care of the district court if I stumble over anything before we stumble over one another again. Like we agreed, the killer or killers have to be riding up and down that steamer line. Nobody's vanished off a day boat going either way, or a night boat headed inland. So I reckon I'll spend the night here in town, catch a day boat up to Sacramento, and ride the night boat back downstream."

Seaforth grinned like a mean little kid and asked, "Might your lady friend in Frisco have a friend for a distinguished older gent?"

Longarm shook his head and declared, "I ain't sure you'd want to meet any of the folks I mean to call upon as long as I'm in town. You told me the Frisco police haven't been able to learn anything from their usual informants. I met some *unusual* informants the last time I was out this way, hunting for some counterfeiters the Treasury boys couldn't seem to find. They didn't want me to find 'em, and you sure get the feel of a town fast when jaspers who know it better are laying for you on the darker streets."

Marshal Seaforth cocked a brow. "We heard about the corners you cut on some of the darker streets of Frisco. I was in mind of your unusual but effective methods when I asked Billy Vail if he'd lend them to us. As you just heard back yonder by that box, the powers that rule don't know

68

shit, and if them sly Orientals know anything, they ain't fixing to let us in on it!''

Longarm smiled modestly and suggested, "It's all in how you ask, Marshal."

To which Seaforth replied, "Do you mean *how* you ask or *who* you ask?"

Longarm said it worked both ways, and ambled off through the hustle and bustle of Frisco's Barbary Coast, which appeared on no official map, but was generally agreed to be the ribbon of total confusion along a waterfront that curved north from Market Street around Telegraph Hill to Fisherman's Wharf and the North Beach, where, as in the case of the Oakland mud flats, it wasn't practical for oceangoing vessels to put in.

Deep-water piers ran out into the bay from a continuous paved strip, broad and narrow, between the piers and slips and the railroad tracks seventy-five or a hundred yards away. That strip along the waterfront was the Embarcadero—or quay in Spanish. From dawn to dusk the Embarcadero was a confusion of freight wagons, low-slung drays meant for heavier tonnage, and carriages, public and private, all trying to get somewhere at once as teamsters cursed, snapped their whips at their teams or one another, and somehow managed to inch through the ongoing jam.

The facilities that had gotten the neighborhood named after a pirate coast of North Africa were the boardinghouses, whorehouses, gambling halls, and grog shops running along the waterfront back from the tracks and the paved Embarcadero. There were some few honest businesses such as ship's chandlers, seamen's shops, hash houses, and such. None of the ramshackle outfits advertising themselves as "Hotels" or "Restaurants" owned up to being anything worse. Strangers to the Barbary Coast had to ask how to find some action. Strangers to the Barbary Coast who advertised they were strangers by asking could wind up beaten and robbed in an alley if they were lucky. They usually were. Blind Boss Buckley, who decided the way Frisco voted, with the help of a sophisticated political machine and a gang of unsophisticated thugs called Buckley's Lambs, frowned on killing tourists outright.

As the half-blind boss who seemed to see everything that went on had once observed to a more greedy cuss, just before they shoved him overboard with an anchor tied around his neck, "You don't sheer sheep by slaughtering them. You fleece 'em gentle, let 'em grow more fleece, and then fleece 'em again!"

But Longarm wasn't looking for a meeting with Boss Buckley this trip. He knew the regular denizens of the Barbary Coast would have tipped the boss off by this time had they ever meant to. So it was likely a safe bet none of the usual Frisco footpads were mixed up in the skullduggery aboard the night boats from Sacramento.

Longarm had another informant in mind as he swung inland a furlong south of the shack-cluttered Telegraph Hill that rose near the north bend of the Barbary Coast.

As he worked his way deeper into a maze of steep narrow streets where children made faces at him, old women stared stonily from their doorways, and no men at all seemed in residence, Longarm was reminded of that old song about Riley's daughter, even though nobody along the slope he was climbing looked Irish. They just looked at him the same way as those Irish folks had looked at the gent in that old song that went:

> As I go walking down the street,
> The paple from their doorsteps blather.
> There goes that Protestant son of a bitch!
> The one who shagged the Riley's dauther!

But he knew that in point of fact the Frisco police were missing some bets by not swearing in any of the Sicilians who'd moved into the old Irish slums from Telegraph Hill to Fisherman's Wharf, off to the northwest. For as in the case of the earlier Irish and Chinese, the Sicilian element of Frisco had its own wise-money boys the mostly honest and hardworking countrymen felt no call to betray to strangers. Folks who offered opinions before they studied on them were prone to claim that this proved all the Irish, Chinese, and Italians could never be virtuous "Real Americans." But the James and Younger boys had never been turned in by the simple country folks of their own Clay County, even after bounties had been posted on them for many a year. A lawman had to get on the good side of some folks before they felt it safe to gossip with him.

Knowing the lady he meant to call on didn't have any known address, Longarm opened the back gate of a small steep patch of fig trees and made sure nobody was following him before he moved on up the slope. It got steeper as you climbed Telegraph Hill.

They called it that because, back in the Gold Rush days, a big old semaphore tower they'd called a telegraph had stood atop the otherwise nameless cone to signal ship arrivals. From the hill you could see ships entering the harbor through the Golden Gate long before anyone in the shipping offices near Market and Montgomery could have. Longarm wasn't sure where they signaled ship arrivals from now that Frisco had filled the whole peninsula with folks perched on higher hills to the west. He wasn't forging his way through all the green figs to ask about shipping news. He was out to see La Strega, which meant The Witch in Italian. But she was really a good old gal if you crossed her palm with silver, and she'd once given him some fine spiritual advice about a suspect the mostly Irish Frisco police had never heard of.

Longarm opened another gate and moved along what seemed a private alleyway to another gate shaded by a grape arbor and leading into a small herb garden rising at an even steeper angle. At the far end, sort of squatting like a toad atop a log, was a low-slung tin-roofed frame house that had never been painted in human memory.

Longarm wasn't surprised when he ducked under the low overhang to find the door wide open to cavernous blackness that smelled of incense and more sinister burnt offerings. He knew La Strega liked to make her visitors uneasy.

He softly called out, "It's Custis Long, ma'am. As you may recall from my last visit, I ain't in the market for love potions or dolis to stick pins in. Where do you want me to sit whilst you materialize at me some more?"

A voice that sounded the way an Egyptian mummy might, if such a sad thing could talk, bade him sit where the rubies glowed. Sure enough, a low divan covered with velvet cushions was suddenly outlined by tiny red pinpoints of ruby light. She'd likely sprung for some of those new photographer's darkroom bulbs since the last time he'd been by. You could run them on wet-cell batteries if you really had any call to, and a sorceress had call to.

So he sat down, trying not to sound impatient as he asked how come they had to go through all this mumbo jumbo again, seeing they'd come to some understandings the last time.

His unseen hostess laughed in a surprisingly girlish tone, and removed the cover of a votive candle between them to reveal herself seated on the far side of a low-slung table covered with black velvet and tarot cards. La Strega was dressed in the same sort of Gypsy outfit with a lot of jingle-jangle that he recalled from last time. But the last time La Strega had looked around sixty or seventy years old. As she regarded him with a catlike expression she looked as mysterious, but not one day over thirty, and way prettier than Miss Mona Lisa with her odd smile.

Longarm feared it might not be polite to ask just what age a lady might really be. And what the hell, the last time they'd met she'd told him she was a real witch.

Chapter 10

La Strega, her granddaughter, or whoever she was waved a dismissive hand to say, "The door behind you is locked and as you know, it is impossible for anyone to move up or down this slope without my knowing of it. As before, you conceal your badge, and this time you do not wear your pistol belt under that same frock coat. But you would not rely on that two-shot derringer alone on a case as important as this one. So you have cleverly concealed a smaller revolver and . . . Enough idle talk. You have come to me once more for information. But this time I fear I have none to offer about criminals of Sicilian extraction."

It would have been rude to tell her he'd had to replace the ready-made tweed suit since he'd had what was called a "cold reading" from a much older woman. He knew how to pretend he knew more than he was letting on too, and it stood to reason no immortal witch or her family could afford to let her die, retire, or whatever when there was somebody with a family resemblance to carry on the family trade. So he told her they'd sent him out her way again to look into those killings or abductions she'd likely noticed in her own cards.

The handsome younger version of La Strega didn't disappoint him. She said, "You are talking about those prospectors who never came back from the Mother Lode. The ones who fanned out from Angel's Camp to pan for color. The ones who bought passage down the river on the Sacramento night boat and were never seen alive again.''

So he knew she'd heard the common gossip along the waterfront, and asked her what her cards had to say about the killer or killers he'd been sent to find. He'd come there hoping a somewhat older witch might have tallied things tighter than the local lawmen. Ladies who cast spells and told fortunes often did. They had to read human nature slick as a whistle to make any money.

The gal he'd decided to accept as La Strega for the time being had been trained to put two and two together quicker than most of the poor souls who came to her for help. She stared earnestly at Longarm and told him, ''The ones you seek have such evil auras it is hard to make much out about them. But I think I see at least one member of the steamer's crew, not creeping like a cat but striding boldly with a friendly but treacherous expression. It is not clear whether he works alone or not. Perhaps if you were to cross my palm with silver . . .''

Longarm reached in his pocket and placed a silver cartwheel in the soft dainty hand she shot across the table. She was a mite more bold, or anxious, this time. She'd likely lost some regular customers after she'd suddenly appeared so young and beautiful. He didn't ask whether older Sicilian ladies had acted jealous or were scared shitless.

Making the coin that was good for a day's groceries vanish, the new and improved La Strega suddenly said, ''You doubt my powers? You dare? How do you suppose I just read your mind if I have no powers, eh?''

Longarm said, ''You're doing fine. Your notion about just one rogue crew member bears looking into. We'd considered a diabolical steam line and decided it sounded too complicated. But one or more deckhands or stewards with the run of the vessels late at night would sure find it easier to get both white men traveling cabin-class and Chinese

74

down on the cargo deck alone for the few minutes it would take to stab, grab, and crawfish back into the shadows.''

Longarm leaned back on the comfortable sofa to add, half to himself, ''We can ask to examine the crew rosters for any company men who might have swapped boat runs down the river with others who might not have felt like staying up so late. When I was in the army we used to spell one another on guard duty or charge of quarters without telling the fool officers. Officers had a way of horning in on an enlisted man who knew where there was more fun to be had near camp.''

She said, ''A white passenger attacked inside a private cabin would be easier for such ruthless people to dispose of. There would be time to tie weights to the body. It would be easier to wait until they knew they were on deep water before they simply opened the cabin door, moved the victim across the narrow dark deck, and rolled him over the rail.''

Longarm placed another silver dollar on the black velvet between them, even though it was his own idea to say, ''There wouldn't be near as much time if the victim was a Chinese sleeping on the cargo deck in mayhaps some nook or cranny. With other honest Chinese within earshot, you'd have to stab, grab, and toss him overboard with as little fuss as you could manage in the few seconds you'd have to work with. We ain't found a survivor yet who recalls waking up to witness a stabbing. What can you tell me about a gal called Tiger Tasha?''

He figured out the mistake he'd made when the cold-reading fortune teller told him, ''That is not her real name. I have to know who I am talking about before I can tell you anything about her.''

Longarm smiled ruefully and said, ''I'm glad I didn't tell you she was a he. But your intuition or whatever is worth your modest fees. She said her real name was Natasha Godanov when I met her on my way out here and noticed she looked as Chinese as Russian.''

La Strega smiled knowingly and said, "You should have been ashamed of yourself for doing such naughty things to a stranger on a train. But your fears she might have been working for one of the six tongs are groundless. None of the tongs are behind those murders up the river."

Longarm said, "A hatchet man I know told me the same thing. Why are you so certain, leaving out cards or crystal balls, ma'am?"

La Strega made a wry face and demanded, "Do you see me dealing the tarot or trying to sell you any other stage magic? We agreed the last time you were here that we were reasonable adults reasoning together. By the way, how did you ever manage to shoot that one suspect in such a droll manner over on the bay?"

She might have made Longarm more nervous if he hadn't met up with professional spooky folks before. He grinned at her in the candlelight and replied, "It was a lucky shot. Us legends have to allow our publics to make what they will of lucky shots. But you were fixing to reveal why I can't arrest any tong boss for all that river piracy."

She said, "The tongs don't operate that way. They seldom rob other Chinese directly, and never attack white men that far from Chinatown if they can possibly avoid it."

Her accent was slipping, so she was likely talking about some mighty serious local gossip when she explained, "None of those prospectors, white or yellow, could have been carrying the sort of wealth a tong leader would take that much risk for. None of the victims owned any serious claims. They were the leftovers of the glory days up in the Mother Lode, panning the low-grade stretches of already prospected creeks for the little color that's always there if you really like to pan and pan and then pan some more."

He said, "I follow your drift. You ain't the first to point out we can't be talking about more than the few hundred dollars worth of dust a free-lancer can pan in six or eight weeks with a whole lot of hard wet work. I'd best put the tongs and Tiger Tasha on the back of the stove for now

76

and look for a crazy-mean killer who kills as much for fun as profit.''

Before he could start to rise, she sensed his shift of weight and said, ''This would be a bad time for you to head back to your hotel. I think you should wait here until the sun goes down and the street lamps are lit. The heavy street traffic and tricky light of quitting time is made for a killer who likes to use a knife, and he knows who you are and that you've been sent all the way from Denver to arrest him.''

Longarm knew how she'd guessed that. *He'd* already allowed for the killer or killers being on the lookout for outside law, having fooled the shit out of the local state and federal lawmen this long. He was working on whether he'd told La Strega last time about that swell hotel he'd found closer to the Ferry Building. Somebody had told her *something,* it seemed safe to say, when she suddenly said, ''I can hide you from your enemies here for as long as you wish.''

Longarm just stared thoughtfully at the suddenly younger witch as he tried to judge the time outside without a rude grab at his pocket watch. She read the uncertainty in his eyes, although not correctly, as she suddenly blurted out, ''What's the matter with you? Do you think I'm still old and ugly? Are you afraid I'm wearing some sort of a mask?''

Longarm soberly replied, ''I never said you were old and *ugly,* even when you looked older, Miss Strega. Where were you when I was talking to your older self that other time, by the way?''

She demurely replied she didn't know what he was talking about. Then she blew out the candle, and those ruby lights around the sofa were switched off as well. So Longarm put a casual hand on the grips of the snub-nosed .445 in a side pocket as he quietly asked her why she wanted things so dark all of a sudden.

Then there was suddenly a perfumed head between his

77

tweedy thighs, and soft skilled hands were fumbling at his fly as Longarm muttered, "Ask a silly question and you're sure to get a surprising answer."

But he hung on to his hidden six-gun as she hauled his more personal shooter, already half hard, out of his pants and hissed, "Be quiet, you fool! I don't do this for my usual clients!"

He managed not to mutter that he sure hoped not as she commenced to play a French horn solo that called for his full attention and a raging erection as she slid her pursed lips down to the roots of his inspired shaft and sort of gargled her wet throat muscles around the head of it until he gasped, "Kee-rist! Let me shuck these duds and do you right! I don't want to waste a come this way, as grand as it may feel!"

And then it felt grander than expected as he came, all the way down to his boots, in the depths of her vibrato as she sort of hummed and swallowed at the same time.

He didn't want to study on how many men a gal would have to suck off before she got that good at it. He'd met many a widow woman who gagged when it got past the base of their tongues. Then La Strega seemed to be pulling his pants down. So he started to unbutton above the waist, but hung on to that .445 just the same as she slithered up to straddle his naked hips with nothing on but her jingle-jangles when he ran his free hand up her smooth flank.

As she slowly but skillfully impaled her trembling body on an old organ-grinder that just didn't seem to know when to quit, La Strega sobbed, "I knew you were this manly and I was so furious at those two other girls you had together at that secluded tearoom!"

To which Longarm could only reply, "I know you and Mr. Barnum's crocodile gal were born many years ago in the shadow of the Sphinx, but you don't know everything. I never bedded those ladies at the same time. One came in to tidy up after the other had gone home, and if it's all the same with you I'd like to get on top and finish right!"

She rolled over with him locked inside her, crossed her bare ankles across the nape of Longarm's neck, and asked, "Why are you still holding that revolver on me, dear? Do you really think I could be this friendly with a mark I was out to clip?"

He laughed and said the thought had crossed him mind, adding, "I trust you a mite more now that you've started to act more natural."

She began to move her hips with uncanny skill as she softly purred, "You'd be surprised how seldom I get to feel this natural. My life or at least a good living depends on my behaving in a *molto respitabile* way in this haunted house. I know you won't believe this. But do you know a lot of my own kind really think I'm older than any of them?"

It wouldn't have been polite to say she sure screwed as if she'd had a hundred years experience, and this close and personal in the dark, he could almost picture her as the sort of sweet-faced old bat she'd been the last time she'd told his fortune. He ran his hand over her soft petite body as he long-donged her, finding her soft but sort of boney ass exciting in contrast with the more robust charms of many a gal who'd gone before her. He'd noticed gals who watched their weight but didn't work or play hard tended to be soft and skinny at the same time. She had big firm tits for her frame, and as many a man knew to his sorrow, two grape-fruit halves on an ironing board often added up to a high-strung bitch who'd screw like a mink one minute and throw things at you the next. But he shoved the .445 into a crack of the velvet sofa to hold her by both skinny buttocks as he let her have his all while she clawed his back, ran bare toes through his hair, and pleaded, "Please tell me they were lying about you and that Chinese whore, Custis!"

He assured her he'd never been near any such person, and this was true as soon as you studied on it. For pretty little Ming Joy worked in a teahouse, not a whorehouse, and he'd never had to pay her.

So a good time was had by all, and when at last they had to come back up for air, Longarm rolled off but cuddled La Strega as he reached for his vest, wherever the hell it had wound up.

The woman crooked in his other arm gasped, "No! Don't smoke in bed with me, Custis. I don't smoke and I don't want you to see me naked."

So he let her have her way, and after a while, she was having her way with his poor old pecker, back on top to slide her tight wet ring-dang-do up and down it like a merry-go-round pony on a big brass rod.

He let her do all the work that time. It was all he could manage to stay hard as she seemed to want to push it past fun into day labor.

But at last she fell off him to flop weakly across the sofa, and when he put out a hand to fondle her, she told him to leave her alone. So he did. Skinny women with big tits were like that. By the time he had his own breath back she was purring, or snoring, like a kitten worn out by its play.

Longarm sat up gingerly, so as not to wake her as he fumbled for his pocket watch and a match. Sitting bare-assed on the edge of the sofa, he thumbnailed a light, saw it was barely after sundown out in the real world, and held the match higher for a fond look at the sweet young thing.

A big gray cat got up to stretch and swish its tail in Longarm's guts as he saw La Strega lying there with one hand on her sated pussy and a pleased smile on her sleeping face.

For while the slender nude body wasn't bad at all, the face was that of the one and original La Strega, framed in white hair and as old as she'd ever looked to begin with!

Chapter 11

The dark foggy slopes of Telegraph Hill smelled like somebody was making clam chowder with a lot of garlic. Somebody probably was. He knew there was a cable car stop less than a quarter mile ahead, but Longarm wasn't ready to catch a ride back to the center of things by way of the high ground, and a good walk in the cool night air figured to clear his head some.

Longarm wasn't superstitious, and he could think of more than one way a gal could look thirty or less in dim light and sixty or more after you'd made love to her in the dark. None of them left him all that sharp-eyed, and they weren't paying him to miss anything as blatant as that! But he had to allow, as he got down to Columbus Avenue and swung south, that La Strega's stage magic had been lots of fun. He'd have never enjoyed her half as much, despite what he now knew to be a whole lot of experience, had he not been picturing her as young and beautiful all the while he was pounding her elderly frame.

Old Ben Franklin had written a notorious letter about older women to a younger diplomat stationed in Paris. Longarm had long since discovered old Ben had been on the money about the way a gal's looks faded some just as she was getting good at fornication. But La Strega had been a tad older than the older women he usually took pity on, bless her dear old juicy ring-dang-doo.

Columbus Avenue came with street lamps, although little else in the way of lighting this close to the north end of town. The few shops along the avenue were closed for the night. The windows were shuttered against the clammy night air and the eyes of prying strangers. But there were a few passing carriages, and now and then somebody shouted something somewhere in the night. So there was just no saying how Longarm figured he was being followed. He just felt he was, the way a deer seemed to sense it was in your sights just before you could pull the trigger. So he stepped into a dark entryway and stuck his right fist in his coat pocket to grip that .445 and see what happened.

Nothing happened. So Longarm moved on, telling himself not to be spooked just because a crazy old witch had cast a love spell on him back yonder.

Columbus Avenue ran at an angle to merge, closer to Market, with Montgomery Street. But that wasn't where Longarm wanted to go. So when he came to what they called Broadway, even though it didn't remind him of any other Broadway he'd ever seen, Longarm veered off Columbus to follow a darker and narrower street toward Chinatown.

If it had a name, nobody had posted any signs on any corner lampposts. There weren't any lampposts, for that matter. The not-too-well-defined Chinatown nestled in the angle of a giant letter L formed by Nob Hill to the west and an east-west-running lower ridge that sort of stuck out of the hourglass figure formed by Nob and Russian Hills like a big fat dick. North-south streets ran over it on the map, but not in point of fact. It was all those dead ends at the end of Chinatown, cutting it off from Downtown Frisco, that made it Chinatown instead of an extension of the main business district along what the local folks called "The Slot," to either side of Market. The center of the city was inland where big old Van Ness Avenue came down from the north, the same as Montgomery, avoiding all the fool hills completely.

Chinatown had street lamps, privately erected, along Grant Avenue and California Street, where they met to form the south gateway to Chinatown. Longarm didn't want too many strangers to know he was on his way to a certain Chinatown jeweler. So he was working his way south in tricky light when he was sure as hell, this time, that somebody was on his tail.

He cut suddenly into what seemed a serviceway between two shut-down storefronts. It led considerably uphill toward the glow of the higher-running Grant Avenue to the west. It doglegged up a flight of steps, and then a street lamp was shining down at him from the top of what he hoped was another flight of stairs.

It wasn't. He'd boxed himself into a blind alley, with eight feet of brick retaining wall and a wrought-iron fence looming between him and the brighter lights so near and yet so far.

Longarm sighed, shrugged, and headed back the way he'd just come with his hand in his coat pocket. He wore low-heeled army boots in spite of such riding as he got to do now and again because a man moved quieter on his feet in well-broken-in low-heeled army stovepipes. So he heard the louder clomping coming toward him in the darkness in time to crawfish back to some trash cans near a dark doorway. He tried the sheet-iron-sheathed door, found it locked, and hunkered down behind the cans, .445 in hand, as a distant voiced called out, "I see yez in there. Come out here and let me be after having a look at yez!"

Longarm stayed put.

The same voice insisted, "Don't be trying to hide your ugly mutt in them shadows, ye scum! I have a gun and I mean to blow your behind off if yez don't stand up with your hands where I can be seeing them while yez tell me what this is all about and all and all!"

Longarm stayed put. The man said he had a gun and he

83

sounded as if he meant it. But Longarm didn't see how anybody was about to fire at him around that solid corner he could make out between himself and a very convincing bluffer.

Then he saw it hadn't been a bluff when yet another voice called out in a worried tone, "Don't shoot, Officer Mahoney! We were just having a little fun with one another back here, see?"

The voice Longarm now recognized replied in disgust, "Aroo, and I don't suppose your mothers ever told you such fun was against the laws of God and man when she was teaching yez to fight with your feet and fuck with your gobs!"

"Don't you be after insulting me poor old mother!" another voice rang out.

To which Mahoney replied without hesitation, "I'll describe your mother as the two-bit whore she aspires to be, and I'd be after insulting your father if anyone on this earth could tell me who the bastard might have been, you depraved cocksucker!"

"Hey, who are you calling a cocksucker?" protested the man Mahoney had so addressed.

Mahoney called back, "If yez ain't up this blind alley queering one another, what else might yez be up to this fine evening?"

Nobody answered. Mahoney ordered them to button their damned pants and come out of there this instant.

They must have. For the next thing Longarm heard was: "That's better, and I have both your names in me little black book now. So be off with yez, and if I find anyone's been broken into around here, yez can commend your souls to Jesus, for your asses will belong to the law!"

As he heard them scampering off, Longarm called out for Mahoney to wait up. He joined the burly copper badge near the entrance of his big mistake. Mahoney laughed and exclaimed, "*Co* Longarm *tha thu,* and what would you have been doing back there with them wayward youths?"

Longarm answered simply, "Trying to get away from them. They were following me. You'd know why better than I might."

Mahoney said, "That's no mystery. You'd be after wearing a suit and thim two would roll their own fathers if they could catch them alone on the street after dark. You don't mean to tell me you'd be roaming the streets in this part of town without that Colt .44-40 you usually pack!"

Longarm explained he was trying to get by with a pocket pistol for now, and as the copper badge walked him to the next corner, he explained what he was working on this time. Mahoney said he'd heard about the boyos never coming back alive from the gold fields to the east. He said the Frisco police had been working on that too. Longarm already knew that, and said, "We just brought another floater down from the delta this afternoon. Everyone seems to agree nobody's been panning enough color lately to pay for a really big gang with some diabolic fiend masterminding the plot. But how do we wind up with no arrests if we're all after a ragged-ass gang of stab-and-grab thugs?"

Mahoney allowed he didn't know, and asked where Longarm was headed.

Longarm said, "I aim to have a powwow with Fong the jeweler. He was a great help to us when I was working that earlier case a spell back. You remember those counterfeiters stamping tolerable twenty-dollar double eagles with fake gold and mighty fine dies, don't you?"

Mahoney said, "I do indeed, and wasn't it yourself who saved the grandfather of Fong Mao? You'd have gotten not a bit of help from that secretive Son of Han if you hadn't been able to put him in your debt forever by saving that older Chink from other footpads and all and all. You know, of course, he's a dealer in stolen goods?"

Longarm said, "The thought had crossed my mind. I'd as soon not have you with me when I pay my call on his back door, no offense. Somebody somewhere must be buying such gold dust as nearly a score of men now have failed to come back alive with!''

Mahoney said, "In that case it's the top of the evening I'll be bidding you, with a note in me little black book that you were last seen on your way to call on Fong Mao, associated with the Hip Sing, and ask if any jeweler in Chinatown would be dealing in goods stolen at knifepoint from at least half a dozen lads under the protection of various darling tongs.''

Longarm said, "I doubt like hell Fong Mao would want to risk his whole family and all they own together for a poke of gold dust. That's how come I want to hear what he has to say about *fencing* the stuff.''

They shook on it and parted friendly on Grant Avenue. Longarm ducked into another service entrance, and negotiated his way through a maze he hoped he had right in his head, while somebody behind him splashed a pan of dishwater out on the cobblestones, and somebody up ahead twanged a one-string banjo and sang like a spring lamb hung up on a bobwire fence. Longarm found a gate that looked about right and opened it to enter a small yard, where some kids played under paper lanterns till they saw a foreign devil coming at them and ran screaming into the house beyond.

A bigger kid with a sawed-off shotgun came outside in his blue pajamas to defend his kith and kin, saw who the foreign devil was, and ran screaming into the house.

Longarm stayed put until, sure enough, the more dignified goldsmith and jeweler, Fong Mao, came outside, holding hands with himself, to bow politely and declare, "I told you before you were welcome to anything you wanted from our humble stock. I see you have finally come back to make your choice. Come inside and have some tea before you make up your mind. We have fine things of ivory, coral, jade, and gold or silver, Deputy Long.''

Longarm shook his head and insisted, "I told you last time I ain't allowed to shake down merchants, Mr. Fong.

Could we talk out here, lest somebody see me inside your shop?''

The jeweler shouted in Cantonese, and some kids materialized with a small tea table and two chairs that they set under a paper lantern. The two grown men sat down as a tea service materialized to be served by a China doll a man might have chosen as a gift had Fong Mao dealt in that sort of merchandise. Longarm paid her no mind, knowing she was likely the older man's daughter, if not one of his wives.

As they sipped green tea with neither sugar, cream, nor handles on the tiny cups, Longarm started to tell Fong Mao about the missing gold dust.

The man shook his head and said, ''You are not the first to ask me about such matters. There are others along Grant Avenue who might buy stolen jewelry, a gold watch, or even gold teeth. But as I told some very concerned *bu how day* who are after the same robbers, few goldsmiths would chance dealing in native gold dust fresh from a placer. Such color is twenty-four-karat, not hard enough for jewelry and too easy to detect as melted-down placer. Any assayer worth his acid could tell within minutes whether a gold ingot or perhaps some jewelry was twenty-four-karat native gold, eighteen-to-fourteen-karat jewelry gold, or anything not refined to such standards in a professional's crucible.''

Longarm said, ''I know those karats stand for the percentage of pure gold to harder metals. Copper for red gold and silver for white gold, right?''

The goldsmith nodded gravely and said, ''Even so. Smelting gold is not a task for a restaurant cook. You don't get jewelry-grade alloys on a kitchen stove with a wok and good intentions. Nobody dealing in gold in San Francisco, of your race or mine, would be dealing in the petty amounts everyone has come to me about.''

Longarm cocked a brow and declared, ''I ain't sure we're talking petty cash here, pard. A hundred dollars here and a thousand dollars yonder does add up in time, you know.''

Fong Mao shook his head and said, "Not soon enough, or simply enough, to justify the risk for anyone running a gold foundry. This may sound odd to you, but men who deal in gold every day become like the men who deal in chocolate, liquor, or women. Those few who can't resist unwise temptations never get rich. They get fat, they get drunk, or they end up married or murdered. I would stake my whole shop on those robbers selling that gold dust somewhere else before I would stake my life on buying even one pinch of gold dust I could not account for!"

Longarm sipped more tea and asked, "In that case, who *might* those murdered gold panners have meant to sell their gold dust to?"

Fong Mao said, "To the U.S. Mint here in San Francisco, of course."

Longarm frowned and said, "Uncle Sam, direct? Not some assay house run by, say, one of the six tongs?"

The doubtlessly paid-up tong member looked pained and told Longarm, "No private assay house would be able to offer more than the U.S. Mint for raw gold. The U.S. Mint sets the price of gold by buying it on the open market, refining, and then coining it at par value. Nobody would pay more than gold is worth as gold specie issued by the government."

Longarm said he was sorry he'd asked. Then he asked, "How might a tong bookkeeper know for certain that a particular member, down from the hills with a poke, sold the gold dust for the price he said he did when they ask him?"

Fong Mao murmured, "It would be dishonest to lie about the modest tribute one owes one's tong. It could even be injurious to one's health if they found out about it, and the U.S. Mint issues a government check, not cash, when you deliver raw gold to them."

Then the courtly older man asked, "What is the matter? Have I said something you did not wish to hear?"

Longarm replied with a sigh, "You sure did. But that's all right. My boss calls what I've been doing the process of eliminating, and so far, you've just eliminated the liver and lights out of a whole bunch of grand notions!"

Chapter 12

No-Nose Brannigan was holding court in a Barbary Coast house of ill repute when Longarm came in by way of a side exit the general public was not supposed to know about. The piano music stopped, but the half-dressed whore on Brannigan's knee was slow to rise, and so she wound up on the floor as the burly Irish bully sprang to his feet and backed into a corner of the downstairs parlor, almost sobbing as he protested, "Whatever it was I didn't do it and I'm not armed, Longarm!"

The taller, leaner lawman kept coming as the crowd of Barbary Coasters and soiled doves parted before him like the Red Sea. No-Nose Brannigan didn't really have no nose. The button he'd been born with had been half erased in a series of brass-knuckle fights, starting at the age of eight or nine. He'd once made the mistake of tangling with Longarm. It had been a mistake he never wanted to make again, and he kept saying so loudly as Longarm quietly cornered him against the red and black paisley wallpaper and calmly observed, "I'm glad to see your bruises have healed so nicely, No-Nose. I haven't come here to kick the shit out of you again. I told you we were square, and I only came to get your views on some even lower lowlifes who've been using knives instead of saps and baseball bats."

No-Nose stared past Longarm, shaking his head and warning, "Don't try it, Hook! It's like the tip of a coach whip he moves and he carries a .44-40 double-action!"

Longarm didn't turn to see how his own back might be doing as he kept covering the gang leader with his palmed double derringer. If they didn't know he'd left his usual six-gun for safekeeping and had a more compact .445 tucked cross-draw in his left boot top, that was their misfortune and none of his own.

No-Nose asked if they could sit down and have a drink together as they talked over old times.

Longarm said, "I just had me some tea and I've never cottoned much to chloral hydrate."

No-Nose protested, "Aroo, and why would I be after slipping knockout drops to a federal man in the good graces of Boss Buckley? You know we'd have never tried to roll you that time if we'd known you weren't a cowpoke who'd wandered north of The Slot!"

Longarm said, "I never came here to chat about old times. Somebody has been stopping other wanderers from getting home from the Mother Lode country by way of the Sacramento Steam Line. Your turn."

No-Nose shrugged and said, "We heard about it. From both the police and the machine. We heard the heathen hatchet men are after the loons as well."

"Why do you call them loons, aside from professional jealousy?" Longarm asked with a sardonic smile. "They've been getting away with it so far."

No-Nose shook his bullet head and replied, "So far would be the fatal words. As we agreed that night we all got some exercise along the Embarcadero, nobody can hope to get away with anything all of the time, and it's a hanging offense to be stabbing a man to death, even if he's a treacherous slant-eyed heathen. Would it be safe to say this is a private conversation between friends, Longarm?"

Longarm said, "Let's not get silly about the way we feel about one another. But I hardly ever record whorehouse conversations in the notes I hand to the teacher."

No-Nose nodded and said, "If me and me boyos were rolling passengers aboard them river steamers, we wouldn't be after *killing* them unless we had to. It's just as easy and not as messy to sap a man from behind as it is to stab him. Once we'd knocked him senseless and helped ourselves to his poke, what would we get out of throwing him overboard, save for a death sentence instead of the twenty years, tops, for armed robbery. And if it please the darling court, who said anything about us bearing *arms* as we were helping the gintleman back to his room after a nasty fall and all?"

Longarm thought some before he answered, "You might not feel quite so gentle if you knew your chosen victim could identify you later."

That had been a statement rather than a question, but the waterfront thug pointed out, "You don't pick a mark who knows you. This world is filled with wealthy strangers. Why go after anybody who can point you out to the law later? It's beginners at the business them river pirates must be, as cruel and bloodthirsty as they are! Could we sit down at least?"

Longarm said, "No. At least one of the victims was found ashore not far from here. It's possible he was stabbed on board and tottered down the gangplank with nobody in the crowd noticing. But it's way more likely they failed to corner him aboard the night boat, followed him off it, and cornered him in that alley instead."

No-Nose said, "We heard about that Chink from the gorl who found him and called the coppers. The poor benighted heathen accused *her* of stabbing him, and it served her right for helping a mark!"

Longarm said, "Nobody thinks she did it. Another dying Chinese said the hunters hauling him into their boat had murdered *him*. But let's not worry about dying men talking

92

silly. Let's stick to who might be behind all this blood and slaughter.''

He let that sink in and continued. ''Footpads trailing one prospector off a boat might trail another. About half of the missing men have never turned up dead or alive. The Chinese victims were mostly riding second-class on the darker cargo deck. Some of them, not all, have been found in the water, mostly up in the inland delta. None of the white men who'd have been sleeping in their staterooms or gambling in the well-lit salon in front of witnesses have wound up floating so far. So what if somebody less gentle than yourself found it easier to get at the Chinese coming down the river, and waited until there came a chance to waylay a white prospector here on the Barbary Coast?''

No-Nose sounded certain as he replied, ''They might get away with it once. They might get away with it twice. But didn't that whore call the law to that alley the moment she found a mark had been hit by some son of a clapped-up tinker without a hunting license? You don't stab marks in another gang's alley. It ain't dacent!''

''Then you know which gang controls the stretch of waterfront where them river steamers put in?'' Longam demanded.

No-Nose replied, ''I do, and you'd be after killing me and me poor old mother before we'd tell you who they are! Sure and I'd be taking a chance with a federal hangman before I'd break the code of dear old Frisco Town! They ain't guilty in any case.''

Longarm thought back to the official report of that known death on shore and nodded, grudgingly, as he said, ''I'll buy those river pirates living by a different code. The hatchet men are pissed off at them too. Is that how come I find you and your boys holed up in here with the girls on a foggy working night?''

No-Nose did not sound sincere as he protested, ''Sure and who'd be afraid of any wild-shooting Chink? It's Buckley's Lambs who've put out the word that the blind boss

93

wants things ever so quiet along the waterfront because he can fix the police but he can't fix you federal men and he knows yez won't go away until things get back to the way he likes them.''

Longarm glanced around at the messy-haired and half-dressed gals in the tawdry gloom, nodded soberly, and allowed, ''He told me one time when I insisted on seeing him that he's not as cruel and greedy as the boss up Oregon way.''

No-Nose made the sign of the cross and answered, ''Ain't that the truth! With business booming this summer and seamen's wages so high that many a skipper will part with as much as eight hundred dollars for a drunk off the docks in condition to learn the ropes or swim ashore as soon as he sobers up on the way to Shanghai! But the boss won't allow shanghaiing along the Barbary Coast lest the army start patrolling around the bend from the Presidio by the Golden Gate. So short-handed ships put in at Portland and ask for a handsome divvel called Bunco Kelly if they need help in the manning of their darling vessels.''

Longarm nodded and said, ''I've heard it wasn't as safe to sleep off a drunk on the paving blocks of Portland. But even if this was Oregon, I'd have a tough time buying that many men being robbed, shanghaied, or whatever in this part of town without anyone else noticing. But keep your eyes peeled and do you see or hear anything, there might be a bundle in it for you. Both the steam line and the tongs have offered bounties at the same time they've been trying to keep the mess out of the papers, hear?''

No-Nose offered to shake on it. But Longarm had to draw the line somewhere. So he just stepped out in the fog, made sure nobody was on his tail this time, and headed for a certain hotel he remembered from an earlier visit. It was closer to the railroad depot in a tidier but not too expensive neighborhood. As he entered around ten-thirty, he noticed a sedately dressed gal seated in an easy chair in widow's weeds and a veiled hat, reading a fashion magazine. She didn't look up as he passed. Still, she seemed sort of familiar. So he was trying to remember where he'd seen her before as the clerk was saying he remembered Longarm from his last visit.

From the way the cuss was smiling, the chambermaid hadn't reported too many spots on the sheets upstairs.

Longarm pocketed the key and headed up the stairwell, pausing on a landing as he sensed he was not heading up alone. He had his derringer out but down at his side, palmed, when that same familiar figure in black came around a bend in the stairway to declare, "It certainly took you long enough to get here, Custis."

Then she reached up to demurely lift her veil out of the way, and that same big cat swished its tail in Longarm's gut again as he saw who it was.

Ticking his hat brim to her, he managed to sound as calm as he told her, "I see you've, ah, recovered some, La Strega. I'd ask you how you do that. But I'm afraid you might convince me, and I just ain't ready to buy black magic, no offense."

As she joined him on the stairs, La Stega barely looked thirty as she pouted, "You ran off and left me sleeping and barely satisfied, you mean thing. But I remembered you'd stayed here with those other girls and . . . Which room is ours, dear?"

He started to tell her there was no way on earth he was going to let such a spooky thing get him alone again. But then he saw they were already alone, and damn that perfume she was wearing, had it only been three or four hours since they'd been going at it so hot and heavy in the dark?

Longarm took a deep breath, let half of it out so his voice would sound less excited, and told her, "I reckon I'm game as long as we leave a lamp lit. I doubt if I could take such a shock again in one night."

She said she didn't know what he was talking about as she took his arm and sort of urged him on up the stairs. He was feeling urgent too by the time he'd ushered her into a plain but tidy room, lit a bed lamp, drawn the blinds, and barred the door. For La Strega was shucking those widow's weeds as if they itched like fire, and she'd been wearing nothing under them, he saw, as she threw herself across the bedstead on top of the covers to fling her silk-sheathed legs high and wide, softly but firmly crying, "Wheee! Ride me, cowboy! Ride me hard and as far as you like, you handsome horny rascal!"

But this time Longarm took his time peeling off his duds, without taking his eyes off her. For there was much worth staring at, all of it a good thirty years younger than the last time he'd seen any of it.

He had the answer as soon as he mounted her deliberately, as if he was a sex maniac playing doctor, and shoved his renewed erection into her warm pulsating wetness. For even as her pelvis rose in welcome and she gasped, "Oh, yesss! It feels even better, this time!" Longarm knew he'd never been in that particular pussy before.

He never said so, seeing that they were so bent on selling him black magic and that it felt so swell. But it was easier to buy a crazy old lady and a crazy granddaughter playing musical cocks in the dark than it was any gal who could change that much in the same night. The family resemblance was tight, as if they'd been twins somehow born in different generations. He'd already recalled what he knew about slender gals with big tits being sort of peculiar, even when they weren't in the magic business.

He was getting used to new pussy when she coyly suggested they put out the lamp so she could try something a little more naughty. He told her he wasn't about to wake up in bed with a lady so . . . tuckered out again. She laughed like hell, and then she blushed all over as he gave it to her dog-style by lamplight. She said she'd never done it that way before. She might not have, not with a lamp lit to afford her bed partner such an intimate view of her twitching rectum. He insisted on some light on the subject when she got on top, but relented when she said she couldn't give French lessons with him grinning down at her.

But once they were in total darkness, he could tell that that was not the same gal from the shack with his dong way down her throat. Not that he had any complaints. The young apprentice witch who'd flimflammed him back on Telegraph Hill didn't suck better or worse. She simply did it different, and thinking back on earlier blow jobs from more than one other gal inspired him so much that she slithered back up to impale her hot young body on it some more as he was coming.

So a good time was had by all, and when La Strega suddenly sat up in bed just before midnight and told him she had to fly off in the night on some mysterious mission, Longarm pretended to be impressed. He might have given his own feelings away if he'd said anything silly about getting across town by broom instead of cable car. He just kissed her *adios,* and made sure the damned door was locked after her lest he wake up in bed with an older witch riding his broomstick.

But it seemed they'd both gotten to screw him, as they'd agreed on, as much as either wanted. So Longarm got some sleep before morning.

But it sure beat all how, riding up to Sacramento aboard the day steamer after such a night, he managed to spend so much of the voyage slugabed in his hired stateroom.

He might have gotten up for noon dinner, had he not known he faced as long a return trip on the night boat, where he didn't intend to doze off or drop his guard for even one minute.

Chapter 13

It would never do to write it down in any official report, but later Longarm would privately decide that it had been just as well two crazy ladies pretending to be one witch had screwed him silly at the western end of the steamer line. For otherwise he might have scouted up an auburn-haired Sacramento gal of Spanish extraction who owned mining property up around Angel's Camp.

But as some cynical French philosopher had observed, a man is complety sane when, and only when, he's just enjoyed a warm meal and a great lay.

Longarm had eaten a swell sit-down supper just before his steamer docked at Sacramento, and he knew that a warm-natured widow with Spanish blood would expect an old flame to show up with passion as well as the usual flowers, books, or candy. As he thought back to the way *her* rump looked by lamplight, he knew he was going to kick himself by the time the night boat was carrying him off downstream. But right then and there it hardly seemed likely she'd know anything important about the free-lancers panning for color well clear of her own hardrock mines. Mine owners worried about high-graders, workers, or trespassers who'd steal color right out of the shaft. They didn't give a shit about an old boy squatting in a creek bed miles away.

He'd bought a round-trip ticket to save standing in line up at the state capital. He had to scurry some to catch the already loaded night boat as it was fixing to cast off. But there wasn't all that much to see in Sacramento to begin with.

He found his luck was holding as soon as he found his stateroom, locked it up even though he had no baggage to steal, and wandered aft to the main salon. For the sun was still shining brightly out on deck as they paddled back away from the pier. And when he asked the barkeep what time they'd dock near the Frisco ferry building, he was told that this was indeed the night boat that got there well before sunrise. The later boat he could have caught, had he looked up a pretty mine owner, would put in to Frisco in broad daylight with heavy traffic along the waterfront. So Longarm ordered a schooner of draft, and lit a cheroot as he found a corner table to sit down at muttering to himself, "This must be the boat. Not a one of the other runs would work as well for me if I was out to stab and grab under cover of darkness!"

It was after supper time, but he knew there was a buffet serving steam-table snacks up forward. He didn't care just yet. He had a long night ahead, and a man stayed more alert without too much swishing around in his gut. He was forcing himself to stay put in one corner as others bustled in and out or paced up and down the promenade outside. Longarm had long since learned, the hard way, that he tended to stand out in any crowd even when he was holding still. He wasn't anxious to become famous on board before he had to. Even a tall man seated in a corner with his hat brim down could sort of fade into the woodwork if he acted quiet but natural. He'd noticed quiet gents who didn't seem to be doing anything at all. You knew such a man was breathing when he smoked and sipped in a calm quiet way.

The late sunlight was lancing in through the starboard

windows of the salon, outlining Longarm as a black but harmless-looking blur, as they headed down the river. Hardly anybody glanced his way as they came in to order drinks and swap stories or tore out to run around the deck some more. It was easy to spot folks who hadn't traveled all that much. They seemed to be having too much fun.

Longarm had decided he'd just come down from Arnold's Camp, higher in the Sierras than most, should anybody ask. When you made up lies, it paid to make up lies that might hold together. Hardly anybody would have been panning for color that far up into tall timber. So nobody was likely to say he'd just come down from there and didn't recall a tall dark jasper called . . . Oh, West Virginia sounded good enough. When you lied about your lawful surname, you could wind up having to explain more than you had time for later. A prospector called West Virginia, scouting the higher slopes for whatever might be up there, covered a lot of bets without sounding interesting enough to worry anybody.

So there Longarm sat, all primed to lie like La Strega, when who should come in but Marshal Travis Seaforth in the flesh.

Worse yet, he spotted Longarm right off, being trained to look the whole crowd over in new surroundings, and came over to say so right out loud.

Longarm wanted to kick him. Instead he said, "Have a seat and let's not advertise. I thought you and Billy Vail wanted me to scout sort of in secret."

Seaforth said, "We did. We do. But I'm too well known along this river to pretend I'm somebody else."

Longarm murmured, "Speak for yourself. I ain't recognized anybody but you aboard this tub and vice versa. Seeing you're so famous, why don't you introduce me around as a mining man you know. Call me West Virginia and disremember anything else about me, save for the fact I ain't wanted by the law and surely know fool's gold from the real thing."

Seaforth said he followed Longarm's drift, and suggested they start a friendly card game to draw a crowd of likely suspects.

Longarm smiled thinly and replied, "You start one and I'll watch on my feet. How many villains have you ever caught knifing a Chinese and tossing him overboard as they were playing cards?"

The older lawman smiled sheepishly and said, "Billy Vail said you thought fast on your feet. But like you said, I'm famous and nobody out to do anything sneaky is going to lose track of *me* no matter where I wander aboard this boat. So what if I play cards in here with my badge and all the lights on whilst you pussyfoot around and see who else don't seem interested in an innocent game of chance?"

Longarm agreed that made sense, but said, "Let's hold off and see if anyone else suggests such a gathering. That ought to eliminate some suspects and give you the chance to introduce me to the crowd as a prospector who may be packing some color before I get tired early and say I'm off to bed. We can likely eliminate some others turning in a mite early because I see at least a dozen men have come aboard with a a female companion."

Seaforth chuckled indulgently and said, "The Sacramento Steam Line has always been famous for its Anchor Beer and moonlight cruises on soft summer nights."

Longarm allowed he'd heard as much and sighed. "No offense, but we ain't likely to find it so romantic after a long tedious night on the river. I say 'long tedious' because I've noticed that ninety-nine out of a hundred times nothing happens when you're standing guard at night."

The older lawman nodded. "That one night in a hundred can be a pisser. I confess I was half asleep on guard late one night when the fucking Modoc struck at last. I haven't dozed off on night duty since. But thank God I'll be getting off at Rio Vista in the wee small hours!"

"You ain't going on to Frisco?" Longarm asked.

The marshal shook his head. "Why should I? I don't

ride for the Frisco District Court. I'm getting off at Rio Vista, if the truth would be known, because I have another place to stay there, this one a boardinghouse run by a widow who's not as young or innocent as my niece, Mairi, at Reedport. Might you be getting off there, by the way, seeing you left all your gear with Mairi?''

Longarm replied, ''Not this run. I'm sure the stuff is as safe with her as it would be with me as I tear-ass up and down this river run. I promised Mairi I'd be back for it all some day.''

By this time the sun was setting, and most everybody drifted out on deck to admire it. You got swell sunsets with a river and a wide flat valley between you and distant coast ranges peeking over a far horizon at you, black as a banker's heart against clouds the colors of banked coals in a fiery furnace. Some of the younger gals on board made Longarm reconsider his own self-control back in Sacramento, now that it was way too late to consider that later run down the river.

''This is the run most of them have vanished from!'' he told himself sternly as a couple who'd been leaning on the rail nearby decided to head back to their stateroom and ring for some ice.

Longarm moved around to the far side to scout the deserted port promenade. He found it as deserted as it was supposed to be, and went down to the cargo deck. Most of the second-class passengers, there being only two classes on that line, were admiring the sunset just like their social betters. But as Longarm sauntered past a bale of hides, a familiar voice calmly asked what he was doing down there among the scum of the earth.

Longarm turned to say, ''Evening, Little Pete. To begin with, I wanted to make sure I didn't have to scout this deck as well. Can I bet on you having all the backing you need down here?''

The young but deadly hatchet man replied, ''Double shift. The Yun Yings have thrown in with us. It ain't nice

102

to grab the fair shares the tongs were banking on. How are you supposed to look out for your faithful supporters if some son of a bitch sticks knives in them and grabs tong tribute?"

Longarm said he almost felt sorry for the river pirates if he or some other foreign devil with a badge didn't catch them first. Then the young highbinder demanded, "Don't you think a man who murders a Ching-Chong-Chinaman deserves to hang?" Longarm could only reply he was sure they'd hang high as hell if he caught them first, but not upside down and skinned alive.

He asked if that tale of a death of a thousand cuts was true, and Little Pete laughed boyishly and assured him, "Shit, the bastards die before the *hundredth* cut most of the time. I like this other trick where they stand the shit over a bamboo shoot spread-eagle on a sort of X-shaped cross. They cut away his pants and shove the tip of the bamboo up his ass, just enough to hurt without really damaging him too much the first day. Then they water the bamboo, and as bamboo will, it grows, and grows some more, a fraction of an inch an hour."

Longarm said, "That sure sounds like fun. I'll be topside if you need me. Call me West Virginia if you have to call me anything."

He went back up to gaze into the salon from the darker side of the steaming vessel. He saw that, sure enough, a card game had just commenced under a lamplit center table with Marshal Tavish Seaforth cutting the cards with a big fat cigar in his face.

Longarm moved up toward the bows and took a lonesome seat in one of the deck chairs they'd set up there. He lit a fresh cheroot and stared eastward at the far higher Sierra Nevadas, the higher peaks still sunlit against a purple sky, with one or two bigger stars turned on already. He knew it would get darker, with more stars, before the moon came up from behind the jagged-ass range. He didn't care.

He'd come aboard to scout for river pirates, not to admire the view.

A feminine figure came around the forward corner of the inward bulkheads, and Longarm didn't care about that either until the gal exclaimed, "Edward! Thank heavens I found you at last! You had me so worried and what are you doing up at this end of the boat, you big silly?"

To which Longarm could only reply, getting up from his deck chair and ticking his hat brim, "I don't have any nicer way to put it, but my name ain't Edward, ma'am."

He added he sure wished it was as he got a better look at her in the tricky gloaming light. She had on a dark print summerweight frock, and her dark hair was pinned up under a bird's nest, or a straw hat pretending to be a bird's nest. The big-eyed heart-shaped face under the silly hat was mighty fine. She might have been blushing. She sure sounded as if she was blushing when she said, "Oh, dear, whatever must you think of me, good sir! I assure you I'm not the sort of girl to talk to strange men I've never been introduced to!"

Longarm said, "Anyone can see that, ma'am. So I'd better introduce myself. They call me West Virginia. You can call me Custis, and I've just come down from the high country with enough color in my poke for a few warm meals and the vaudeville show at the Jenny Lind Theater before I head back up to a placer I don't know you well enough to brag about."

She said her name was Sally Speedwell, and didn't want to tell him who in blue blazes "Edward" might be.

As they stood there awkwardly on the gently rolling deck, Longarm gently told her, "I know it's none of my beeswax, ma'am. But if this Edward cuss has somehow let you down . . ."

She started to cry.

It seemed only natural to take the poor thing in his arms politely, as if he'd been her big brother, and say soothingly,

"You don't have to tell me anything personal. Just tell me how much it might take to get you out of this fix you seem to be in, Miss Sally."

That inspired her to bury her face in his vest and blubber some more. He told her, "I'm sure old Edward never meant to miss the boat on purpose, Miss Sally. Which end of this run do you live at?"

She sobbed, "San Francisco. I should have known better. He told me we were only going to enjoy a pleasant outing up the river. I was so surprised when he tried to force his way into my stateroom on the way up to Sacramento. But I thought we had it all settled when he apologized and promised to make it up to me on the return trip. I can't understand where he could have gone. He said he'd meet me back at the boat and . . ."

"There's another boat leaving later tonight," Longarm told her. He patted her trembling shoulder and repeated his offer of financial help. To begin with, he wanted to give her some rope. And for all he knew, the pretty little thing could really be in a fix.

But she said she was booked downstream on a return ticket, and assured him she'd been smart enough to bring along enough money to see her home older and wiser.

Then she asked if he'd walk her to her own stateroom. So he did, reminding himself to shove that .445 deeper into his boot top as soon as he got the chance.

They got around to her door on the port side. She opened it and stepped inside to turn and face him with a shy smile, the light being better on that side of the steamer. She sure looked pretty as she told him, "I'd invite you in for a drink, Custis. But it wouldn't be proper and it wouldn't be fair to you. I don't set out to tease men, but they all seem to feel I do for some reason."

Longarm smiled down at her and replied, "I know the reason. I reckon some gals just can't help it. But I won't pout and I won't cry and your Edward is a total fool."

She laughed, told him he was awfully sweet, and shut the damned door in his face.

So there went a couple of grand notions about ulterior motives, and there he stood with a dumb grin on his face and a whole tedious night on the water ahead of him!

Chapter 14

The night got even longer and more tedious as it wore on. For as every soldier who ever stood guard duty could tell you, waiting and watching for something to happen when nothing was happening made a minute seem like an hour.

Your eyes didn't gum up as soon when you weren't afraid to doze off, sitting up aboard a train or stretched out in a deck chair. You could kill lots of time allowing your mind to wander, not caring whether a daydream drifted into the real thing. A man could spend a lot of time, unless he'd led a sheltered life, trying to add up all the gals he'd had without a pencil and paper. He'd usually recall he'd skipped one a few towns back, have to retrace, and with one pleasant memory after another, kill an hour or more before it came time to consider who he'd lay first if his dirty fairy godmother gave him his choice of every actress ever featured in the *Police Gazette*.

But a sentry gathering wool or jerking off was a sentry made for raiders or horse thieves to get past. So Longarm had to stay on the alert as the boat steamed through the moonlight hour after hour and not a fucking thing seemed to be happening.

He hadn't heard anybody fucking as he passed their stateroom for a good while, and most of the players had left that card game in the main salon, too tired or too tapped out to sit up any longer.

Longarm had been tempted to join in as things got ever quieter in all the other places he could wander with a cheroot in his teeth and that .445 in his boot. But he knew that once you got into a game, the only graceful way to quit called for leaving the scene completely.

So he was leaning against the bar, nursing another beer as he ate peanuts one at a time and watched Marshal Seaforth yawning and dealing at the same time, when a scrawny old coot he'd noticed pacing restlessly around the promenade earlier bellied up beside him to wake the barkeep up by ordering a bourbon with branch water.

Longarm didn't say anything. A man avoided a lot of barfights by letting others decide whether they wanted to talk to him or not.

The old coot put away half his drink and turned to lean his own elbows on the bar as he quietly observed, "I see somebody told you about Tiger Brand playing cards too."

There was nobody at the bar but them. So Longarm decided it was safe to answer, "I've been warned more than once not to buck the tiger. But to tell the pure truth, I ain't sure why one brand's worse than any other."

The old coot never called him a big fibber. He said, "It's all in the tiger's tail. Nobody would be dumb enough to alter the stripes on the tiger's back with India ink. But the skinny tail's more a dotted line of black and yaller nobody hardly looks at. So do you ink out a yellow dot here, there, or yonder, it's hard for the rest of us to spot, and meanwhile there's enough bitty stripes on the tiger's tail to indicate all the high cards, see?"

Longarm tried to sound like a hayseed as he replied, "I surely do. Nobody needs to mark any low cards, save for aces and deuces, unless the game is rummy. So my momma was right when she told me never to buck tigers!"

The older man laughed easily and allowed his name was

Farnsworth, D. J. Farnsworth, and all his friends called him Doc.

It wasn't easy, but Longarm resisted the temptation to say momma had warned him to never play cards with any man called Doc either. It made more sense to just tell the old coot they called him West Virginia.

Doc let that digest a spell before he allowed that the marshal yonder had said old West Virginia was a sourdough down from the hills with a poke.

Longarm allowed he'd already cashed in his color at the assay office in Sacramento. You had to think ahead when you were lying to others.

Doc said he'd been up around Murphy's Camp recently, and asked if West Virginia recalled the name of that Wells Fargo stop in that big two-story 'dobe between Murphy's and Angel's Camp.

Longarm said he didn't even recall the winner of the last frog jump down in Angel's, and added, "I've been up around Arnold's Camp this summer. There's a hardrock shaft still producing near Murphy's and Angel's, but there's been many a spring flood and many a Chinese through all the original placers you can get to easy."

Doc said he hadn't heard of all that much color in the higher slopes of the Sierra Nevadas. Longarm told him, "Gold is where you find it, and it wouldn't be worth as much if you always found it where you'd expect. Before you hit me for a loan, Doc, I never said I'd found that much anywhere. I panned just enough to pay for a two-week vacation in town. Some old boys work in town all year and take two weeks off in the country. In my line of work it's the other way around, and the few bucks I made with a whole lot of panning is mine, all mine!"

Doc laughed easily and said, "Your momma taught you well about the perils of civilization, West Virginia. I ain't after your poke or even your fair white pecker. I'm just a lonesome old fart who's never been able to sleep worth shit on a bunk that won't hold still."

Longarm allowed that made two of them as he faked a yawn. Doc said, "I understand we'll be putting into the Frisco docks before sunrise. I hate to get up that early when I have someplace to sleep. I hope a pal I wired from Sacramento is an early riser. I asked him to meet me at the pier with his shay. *Walking* in that part of town at that time of the morning can get mighty spooky."

He let that sink in, and said, "You don't have anybody waiting for you on the pier, I suppose?"

Longarm shook his head and said, "I figured on walking direct to Market and following the street lights to the Palace Hotel."

Doc smiled thinly and said, "You *did* pan some color up by Arnold's, didn't you? You naturally have somebody special waiting for you at a hotel that fancy?"

Longarm grinned dirty and said, "Not nobody special. Half the fun is having one's pick of the debutantes you meet there. That's what a fancy gal calls herself when she can afford to stay at the Palace—a debutante."

Doc said he'd heard Dirty Mary's up the other way was way cheaper, with good liquor and fine-looking gals who bathed regular. Then they made more small talk until Longarm said he had to get some fresh air. He knew nobody was going to try and rob him in the main salon with a U.S. marshal as only one of the witnesses.

But though he circled the promenade half a dozen times, alone in the dark with his derringer palmed, nothing happened. Could he have misjudged Doc? Windy old coots you met while traveling didn't always want to rob you or suck your cock. Sometimes they were just windy old coots.

He moved down to the cargo deck to find most everyone asleep on the deck or propped against comfortable cargo. Up in the dark shadows of the starboard side-wheel box, a familiar voice confided, in the tone of a friendly graveyard haunt, "I wish you'd stay the fuck topside, Round Eyes. I've been imitating a clear coast for over an hour here.

110

Who's going to make his move with a stray moose running up and down the deck?''

"I came to compare new notes," Longarm replied. "Another sinister squirt just made me remember that assay office back there in Sacramento. How come your Sons of Han risk hauling their gold dust all the way down the river to Frisco?''

Little Pete said, "Two reasons. Cash would be even easier to steal and get away with if we're talking about river pirates. And half a poke can be sold at the assay office under one name and half under another if we're talking about fucking Chinamen who all look alike."

Longarm started to ask a dumb question. Then the answer sunk in and he said, "Right. A lad with larceny in his heart could present just the receipt he got for half his dust, sold under his own name, and never pester his tong about the other half or more he sold under the name of . . . what's the Chinese for Smith?''

"Wong," said Fung Jin Toy, dryly adding, "When you add it up, the most numerous human being on this earth is a Chinese woman named Miss Wong. But who'd know that at your average assay office, and like I said, it would be easier to get away with cash no matter who was out to screw whom."

Longarm said, "Fong the jeweler told me the tong treasurers pass the raw gold on to the U.S. Mint in Frisco. Are the two of you any kin, by the way?''

Little Pete snorted, "Can't you hear the difference between Fung and Fong? Is *shitting* a gun the same as *shooting* it? I don't know what they do with their fucking gold dust once they get hold of it. They've only asked me and my boys to make sure it gets to them!''

"Don't get your bowels in an uproar," Longarm said, reminding himself that the hatchet man was younger and likely greener than he wanted others to think. "I'm trying to shave away possibles till we get down to way more likely. What if I was a hardworking Son of Han who just

111

didn't want to share that much with my tong and so I took my dust to the assay office in Sacramento, sold *some* of it under a name not my own, and tore up the receipt?''

Little Pete said, ''I'd rather commit suicide by stretching out on an anthill under a hot sun. To begin with, the tongs have branches up in most of the mining camps as well as Sacramento. We may all look the same to *you*. But a Chinese who went anywhere near that assay office could wind up explaining why he'd gone anywhere near that assay office, with lit bamboo splinters under his fingernails.''

Longarm smiled grimly and said, ''You're doing fine. We just eliminated *that* notion. Fong the jeweler eliminated another when he convinced me how hard it would be for a Chinese to sell his raw gold anywhere else in Frisco. But if he was willing to sell a tad below the going price, to, say, some white prospector who could take it to the mint for—''

''You're chasing your own tail,'' Little Pete cut in with another snort of disgust. ''It doesn't matter whether anybody intended to cheat their tongs or not. Somebody else keeps killing them and taking whatever the fuck they have on them! Nobody is keeping books on the exact amounts of missing gold dust. A dead gold prospector is never going to bring in any gold at all, see?''

Longarm did, and Little Pete's point about him discouraging any other night prowlers just by prowling down there was well taken. So Longarm went back up to his own deck, took a turn around it without a nibble, and saw by shore lights that they were coming in to Rio Vista. So he moved back to find some crewmen ready to lower the gangplank, and sure enough, Marshal Seaforth was standing by with a couple of others getting off there.

There was time for them to compare notes as the steamer made her way to the landing. Longarm asked Seaforth if he knew anything about the windy old coot who called himself Doc.

The older lawman said, ''We call him Doc too. He's a

112

regular on this run. Whiskey drummer. A real one. I made sure he reps for a couple of well-known brands after I'd noticed him aboard a night boat more than once.''

Longarm said he was glad to see great minds ran in the same channels, and told the older lawman he'd about given up on this particular run.

But when Seaforth agreed things seemed quiet and suggested he pack it in for the night, Longarm shook his head and said, "You only have to stay put in the duck blind one minute longer than the ducks take to get there. Knowing I ain't Doc's intended target, I'll likely manage to pussyfoot about even better.''

The boat had put in and they were lowering the gangplank. So the two lawmen shook on it and wished one another good hunting. Old Seaforth had as much as said he meant to get laid in Rio Vista.

Somebody else was getting laid in the stateroom next to the one Sally Speedwell lay alone in, if that Edward cuss had really ditched her up Sacramento way. Pausing by the ventilation jalousies, Longarm heard a female whisper pleading, "Not in there, Huggy Bear! You know I love you, but it *hurts* when you insist on treating me so Grecian!''

Longarm grimaced and moved on, wondering if the gal he'd escorted to the next-door stateroom was awake and listening. Then he couldn't help wondering whether hearing others rutting in the nearby dark had the same effect on her as it had on him. That gal who didn't like to take it in the ass could be fat and ugly for all he really knew. But he sure felt left out as he moved on, willing to screw her the way she preferred, whoever she was and whatever she might look like.

He went to his own stateroom to sit on his berth and take a break. But he didn't lie down or jerk off. He just needed time to think without feeling tensed to fire his derringer and drop down to one knee for a grab at his hidden backup. He put the double derringer aside on the berth, and reached

113

down to pull up a pants leg and cross-draw the ugly little English six-gun and check the five rounds in the wheel. The peculiarly British .445 caliber reminded him of the needlessly complicated way the British coined their money, with half-penny, two-penny, or three-pence coins to go with their plain old pennies. They priced high-toned goods in guineas instead of pounds because the hoi polloi could add twenty-shilling pounds as forty shillings, sixty shillings, and so forth. But a one-pound-plus-a-shilling guinea made it tough to say what your fancy carriage had cost, and maybe a common cuss getting hit with a .445 would be impressed by the extra fraction of a fraction of an inch.

The English calibrated their bullets to the same inch Americans measured with, .25-caliber being a quarter-inch, .50-caliber half an inch, and so forth. American gunsmiths felt no call to split less than a hundredth of an inch. So a plain old .45 round was five one hundredths of an inch less than .50 caliber, or forty-five percent of an inch in diameter. So why in thunder did the folks at Webley have to be so picky?

Nobody told him. But stewing about needless complications got his juices flowing again, and he went back on deck, and a million years later they were putting in at Reedport and he got to think about pussy some more, even though it would have been one hell of a time to wake up a gal with copper-colored hair.

Then he noticed there was a crowd on the pier, with some torches waving and lighting up a supine figure wrapped in white sheeting. It looked as if somebody had been taken sick or shot and needed to get to a hospital in Frisco fast.

Longarm moved aft to see who they'd be bringing aboard, hoping like hell it wasn't a young widow with copper-colored hair.

Chapter 15

It wasn't. Longarm didn't recognize the young jasper they brought on board lashed to an improvised litter. Given that tricky light and the condition his battered face was in, his own mother might not have recognized him. Someone had surely worked that boy over and likely stomped on his head. Longarm didn't want to be spotted and identified by any of the Reedport crowd. So he hung back and just listened as the country doctor taking the battered boy to Frisco for some surgery explained it to the steamer's purser.

The purser was the officer who said who got on or off and where he wanted them and their belongings to go on board. The one on duty that run allowed they could carry the battered boy up in officers' country on the Texas deck. Trailing along in the wake of the gathering crowd of other passengers, Longarm heard one of the old boys from the shore explain that the beating victim was a farm boy who'd paid court to the one true chosen love of the hard-riding Miwok Mason. When a passenger asked how come nobody had arrested such a brutal cuss, the Reedporter told him that was easier said than done. To begin with, old Miwok tended to ride home and fort up after he'd hospitalized a lesser man who'd crossed him. After that, there wasn't any town marshal in Reedport and neither the county nor federal lawmen who came by now and again seemed to feel the local bully was worth their while.

A Reedport hand who'd been holding back snorted in disgust and opined, "Nobody's afraid of old Miwok in the flesh. But you have to get past his hired guns to arrest him, and after you arrest him his hired political fixers always get him off."

The first one replied, "That's what I just said. Why risk your ass taking a spoiled rich kid with friends in high places? They say he killed a man all the way up by Red Bluff. Old Lefty's lucky Miwok and his greasers didn't kill *him* tonight!"

Longarm fell back and waited alone in the bows until the hands who were going ashore went ashore and the steamer got under way again.

Then he mounted the forbidden stairs to the Texas deck, and when a deckhand on duty there told him he wasn't allowed in officers' country, Longarm flashed his badge and said, "Sure I am. Don't give me no shit if you want to steam up and down a federal waterway and don't tell the other paying passengers you ever saw this badge."

The deckhand said he wanted no trouble with Uncle Sam, and when Longarm asked, he told him which way to go from there.

Longarm found the purser and the country doctor in a spartan but sanitary cubbyhole between the funnels. A steward was standing by with a big copper bowl of cracked ice. The doc was dabbing at the cut-up and swollen features of the boy called Lefty with a wet towel and an ice pack. The purser asked what Longarm thought he was doing there in the doorway.

Longarm said, "They pay me to be nosy. I ride for the law. Federal. I understand we got us a love triangle gone to assault and battery here."

The badly beaten Lefty protested, "Warn't no love to the infernal way that maniac and his greasers treated me! I never messed with his old widow woman. Miss Mairi must

116

be close to thirty years old, for Gawd's sake! I told him I wasn't the least bit interested in her, and he claimed I'd insulted her and deserved to be made an example of!''

The doc chimed in. ''We're not going to save this right eye if we don't reduce the swelling fast! The son of a bitch broke the orbit and sphenoid bones with a gun barrel while the boy was being held by those greasers!''

Longarm quietly asked if they were talking about the California brand of greaser or the old Mexico brand of greaser.

Lefty smiled as bitterly as his puffed lips allowed and said, ''If you was being helt by greaser whilst their boss pistol-whupped you, would you ask them to show you citizenship papers?''

Longarm nodded soberly and replied, ''Yep. Might make a powerful difference in a court of law. We'll talk about it later, once you're up to pressing charges and I'm free to pay a call on the bully of your town.''

Lefty said, ''Forget it. Siwash Anderson pressed charges the time Miwok and his riders roped and drug his outhouse with his daughter in it. The county let Miwok off with a fine he could afford, and the next thing the Andersons knew they didn't live there anymore. They were lucky to get out of their house alive when somebody set it afire in the wee small hours!''

Longarm started to ask if Lefty and the others were willing to let one rich man and a handful of hired guns ride roughshod over them as much and as long as they felt like. But when you asked dumb questions you got dumb answers. So Longarm said, ''Have it your own way. Or at least Miwok Mason's way. They only pinned a badge on me. Not a suit of armor and a crusader's cross.''

He went back down to the promenade to get back to his own chores, circling the empty deck in the predawn chill in hopes of getting a nibble while he mostly got more tired and, by this time, hungry.

The forward dining salon was dark and shuttered, but he

117

heard the sound of pots and pans being moved about inside. So he knew they'd be serving breakfast before cock's crow. There was no way to eat breakfast by daylight on this run. There was only a bare chance that longer stop at Reedport might keep them from beating sunrise over the Frisco Bay.

He went back down to the cargo deck, as much to kill time while his stomach felt so growly as to see if any Chinese had been murdered.

None of them had. Little Pete looked as tired and hungry as they compared notes at the foot of the forward stairway. Longarm opined, and the hatchet man agreed, that there was no way to predict the next move of a dedicated sneak. Longarm said that they were on the right track, if they just kept retracing the same moves up and down the river. Little Pete said he was really looking forward to a life on the bounding wave.

Then, at long last, they flung open the doors of the dining salon and Longarm charged inside, inhaling the grand smell of waffles, fried pork sausages, and fresh-brewed coffee.

They served breakfast cafeteria-style. Longarm ordered extra helpings, and carried his tray to a table near a window to admire the pitch blackness outside. He knew they had to be somewhere on San Pablo Bay by this time, even though the bigger steamer didn't bob the way that small launch had. He'd demolished most of his waffles and sausages when a familiar voice trilled, "I see I'm not the only starving orphan aboard this vessel. Those waffles smell delicious!"

Longarm rose from his own bentwood chair and told Sally Speedwell to sit while he fetched her some. She said she took cream and sugar with her coffee, and when he got back to their table with her breakfast just in time, she insisted on sliding some money across the fake marble at him.

He didn't want to argue in front of the others crowding in now. He saw that other doc who sold whiskey, and had to nod. To his credit the old coot knew better than to carry his own tray to their table and horn in. But it was easy to see how gents such as Miwok Mason might feel about extra company at times such as this. He found himself idly wondering whether Miwok and Miss Mairi had ever eaten breakfast together like this, or which of the two gals might be easier to get in bed with.

He'd never made a move with Mairi Seaforth, her being the niece of a plain-spoken as well as older lawman. The darker gal across the breakfast table from him made the first move. Or at least she gave a man the chance to make his own first move when she asked if he'd be met by anyone at the dock when they got to Frisco.

He told her the same tale he'd told Doc Farnsworth earlier in the main salon. It was the simple truth. He hadn't made any detailed plan of escape from the Embarcadero. That one Chinese had been followed off the boat at least that far. He told Sally it would likely be daybreak by the time they pulled in. She said she sure hoped so. He was lying like a rug when he said *he* hoped so too.

The brunette who said she'd been ditched by a boyfriend for saying no said she'd never been down around the Embarcadero unescorted night or day. Longarm tried to let that pass over his head. But she looked as if she was fixing to cry if he didn't take the hint.

So Longarm said, "I'd be proud to see you and your baggage clear of the docks and on your way home by hired hack, Miss Sally. How far do you have to go once we get there?"

She said, "Rincon Hill, just south of Market Street but a world away from the Barbary Coast. I mean, I can see the bay from my bedroom window, but for some reason there are no saloons and such along the waterfront south of The Slot."

He said, "There's a good reason. Miss Sally. Only a few oceangoing ships put in to the slips of those sugar refineries, coffee-roasting plants, and such down your way."

She said she didn't know much about ships, and asked

119

him if he was by any chance a seaman, adding she'd have taken him for a cowboy.

He almost told her who he was. But there was no telling who might overhear, or who a sort of skittish young thing might blab to. So he told her, "I used to herd cows. Prospecting pays better with no partners to split with, even when you pan worked-over tailings. I know the little I do about the Frisco waterfront because I get into town now and again, when I've had enough of the wide-open spaces."

She said, "Surely you don't spend all your time in San Francisco along the Barbary Coast. Don't you know any nicer people in town?"

He told her truthfully he didn't get in to Frisco too often. So she sighed and said, "I wish you had the time to let me show you some of the finer features of San Francisco. I'd love to nibble like this with you in the Cliff House, overlooking the Pacific, or perhaps you'd rather visit the art museum on Van Ness Avenue."

He let himself sound dubious as he replied, "I ain't much for high-toned sightseeing, ma'am."

She dimpled at him and insisted, "You never know what you like before you've given it a try. It's settled, Custis. After you've seen me home to Rincon Hill, I insist on you letting me improve your mind with a guided tour of San Francisco."

Then she looked sort of archly at him over the rim of her coffee cup and softly added, "After we've both rested up from this trip, of course."

He said that sounded reasonable. But hadn't she told him she'd said no to that *other* jasper?

By the time it was getting light outside and he could see they were headed due south down Frisco Bay, Longarm had decided that "Edward" had been awfully ugly, awfully awkward, or nonexistent.

That seemed only fair. Hardly anybody ever just came right out and said they liked your style and wanted to play slap and tickle with you. Gals had the same rights as men did to make up tales of woe, and being ditched by an Edward was no worse than saying one's wife just didn't understand one.

They beat the sunrise to town, but not by much. Longarm had no baggage this trip, and it only took them a jiffy to fetch her one overnight bag from her stateroom. An idiot named Edward or anything worse might have grabbed the pretty little thing for a feel and some spit-swapping as soon as they were alone in there. Longarm knew they'd be docking before the good slap he'd deserve stopped stinging. So he behaved the way she said Edward had been too eager to behave, and less than twenty minutes later, they were crossing the damp cobbles of the Embarcadero in a morning mist that didn't tie up traffic as the morning rush got under way.

He told her to stand on a curb across the way while he hailed them a hack. But she said they'd never get one at that time of the morning, and offered to walk if he'd tote her one bag.

So that's how they got her home, to a canary-yellow and brick-red frame near the crest of the smaller and less famous Rincon Hill just south of The Slot.

Sally said it felt good to be home, and bade him act as if he belonged there while she changed. As she picked up her overnight bag she told him she'd be right back to make him that drink he'd turned down the night before.

He never said it had been her notion to slam the door in his face, for the same reason he didn't ask her what the big hurry was. Queen Victoria doubtless took an occasional piss after two cups of coffee and a long uphill walk. But she never said that was where she had to go when she said she'd be right back.

Longarm hung his hat near the parlor door, and strolled over to a lace-curtained window that gave him a better view of a big brick warehouse than any bay. She'd said you could see the bay from her bedroom. So that was something else to look forward to.

She wasn't there to give him her permission to smoke, and he saw no ashtrays in any case. He sat back down, yawning on purpose this time. It had been a long night and he'd planned on catching another boat back to Sacramento after a few hours sleep.

But there'd be a later boat or, hell, no boat at all for a while if things worked out right with old Sally.

Smiling softly, Longarm muttered, "I know what you're thinking, and you're likely right about me, Billy Vail. On the other hand, she has offered to introduce me around to her own class of folks. So far, most of the Frisco folks I've met have been sort of lowlifes, and it might pay to meet up with some middle-class white jewelers as well."

From the next room Sally trilled, "I'm almost decent! Do you take water with your rum or on the side, Custis?"

He called back he'd rather cut his own rum. When gals made rum drinks, they tended to put sugar and all sorts of shit in it if you didn't watch them.

In the other room, having made herself comfortable in a black cotton kimono, Silken Sally Sullivan, as she was better known to her friends and relations, wasn't putting sugar in the heroic drink she was pouring for her mark. She was glad he'd asked for his rum neat. It was Jamaica rum with a powerful smell and a natural punch. So she could put plenty of chloral hydrate in it, and the big moose in the next room looked as it would take a double dose to knock him galley west.

Chapter 16

Longarm saw what she'd meant by changing to something comfortable when the gal he knew as Sally Speedwell came back in with the fixings on a teakwood tray. The kimono was sashed at the waist, but didn't seem to have any buttons up or down, and she sure was a hairy little thing.

But he pretended not to notice, lest she spoil the view, as she sat down on a tufted leather chesterfield with him and set her tray on the low coffee table.

He saw she'd provided a jug of rum, a pitcher of ice water, and a bowl of Italian breadsticks. She'd already poured a couple of jiggers of tea-brown rum over the ice in his glass, and topped her own off with water to where it sort of looked like iced piss.

Longarm leaned forward to water his own drink as she reached for a breadstick, seemingly unaware of how much thigh was showing when she leaned back to sort of suck it off while she waited to clink glasses from the looks of things.

Longarm raised his glass to his lips, sipped, and declared that that was sure strong stuff, then put it back on the tray to fill it up as high as her nearly full glass.

She took the wet breadstick from her sensuously smiling lips to ask if he'd like a taste of that as well.

Longarm reached for his glass, saying, "I can still taste all them waffles they served us on the steamer. But mayhaps your pet squirrel would like one."

She stared blankly at him. "Pet squirrel? I don't have a pet squirrel. I don't have any pets at all up here."

He smiled at her uncertainly and asked, "You don't? Then what was that cute frisky critter as just scampered along the baseboard and under this very sofa?"

Sally yanked her slippered feet from the rug as if it was on fire, affording him an astonishing view before she wound up on her knees atop the tufted leather, gasping, "I don't have mice! I *won't* have mice! I can't *stand* mice!"

Longarm said, "Aw, it wasn't no mouse, Miss Sally. I never got a good look at it. But if it wasn't a squirrel, it was about the same size and color as a squirrel."

She blanched and declared, "Oh, my God, one of those horrid wharf rats from the sugar works! Why are you just sitting there? You're the man! You're supposed to *do* something!"

Longarm smiled sheepishly and rolled off the chesterfield to kneel beside it and shove the table clear as he fished out his derringer.

Sally protested, "You can't fire that gun in here, you big oaf!"

Longarm replied, "I sure ain't about to reach under this sofa with my bare hand! Do you have a broom I can poke around with down here?"

She jumped off the chesterfield, ran to a nearby closet, and got a dust mop instead. She stayed well back from Longarm as she gingerly held one end out to him, pleading, "Don't squish it. Just drive it away and I'll have the landlord set some traps downstairs. I can't stand squished creatures!"

So Longarm lay the double derringer on the table and bent low to probe around under the sofa with the mop handle until he finally told her, "It seems to be gone. Must

124

have run out from under us whilst you were bouncing on your pretty knees above it.''

She fluttered her lashes, and moved hesitantly to rejoin him as he pulled the coffee table closer, sat down, and picked up his glass. She sat down beside him to pick up her own, raising it high to gallantly offer, ''Here's to Mr. Rat, wherever he went.''

So they clinked and sipped at their drinks at last. Longarm hadn't known his mouth felt that dry before he'd wet his tongue with the cooling refreshment. He told her so, and that seemed to make her laugh for some reason.

Longarm sipped some more and set his glass aside, three-quarters gone, so he could lean back expansively and confess, ''I know you said you wanted to show me the Pacific Ocean and such, Miss Sally, and I know you feel like you just got up. But to tell you the truth, I was up all night aboard the steamer, and right now I'm having a tough time keeping my eyes open, no offense.''

She demurely replied, ''None taken. Would you care to stretch out and catch forty winks? I could always do my nails or something.''

Then she yawned, blinked, and added, ''As a matter of fact I could use a few winks myself, and I did get plenty of sleep aboard that night boat. I can't understand what's come over me!''

Longarm calmly told her, ''It smelled like chloral hydrate, ma'am. As you know, it wouldn't be so popular with gals like you if it had a really strong taste or smell. But once you know the smell you don't forget it. So I reckon you ain't used to drinking your own knockout drops, eh?''

She stared at him owl-eyed, tried to rise, then sank back weakly as she sobbed, ''Bastard! You switched glasses on me!''

To which Longarm modestly replied, ''Had to, unless I wanted to drink that sleeping potion my ownself. But look on the bright side. You don't really have rats and whether you live or not depends on how much you meant to give me.''

"Call a doctor!" she sobbed. "I put enough in the glass to knock out a big moose like you and I'm so tiny!"

Longarm smiled fondly at her and said, "When you're right you're right, and it might help if we were to make you puke some before you passed out. So tell me how come you treated me so considerately after you'd stabbed all them Chinamen, and I'll mix you up an emetic, hear?"

She yawned, gasped for air, and sort of burbled that she didn't know anything about any Chinamen.

He picked up the derringer, in case she was faking, and rolled her off the chesterfield to lie flat on her back. Her kimono was open, but this was no time to charge her with indecent exposure. He went into her kitchen and rummaged around till he found some powdered mustard and a bar of castile soap. She had indoor plumbing. Serving knockout drops to fellow travelers seemed a profitable occupation. He mixed up his own potion of soapy mustard water and carried the mug back to where she now lay blowing bubbles out her nose.

He hunkered down, propped her head up, and got her to sip a little of his simple but effective emetic. She gagged and blearily told him it tasted like shit.

He insisted, "It's good for what ails you and you *deserve* to eat shit, you murderous little thing."

He got more of it down her before she suddenly retched and would have puked all over him if he hadn't turned her head the other way to let her soil her own rug. He made her swallow and puke some more before she managed to burble, "I'm not murderous. I'm only greedy. Why do you keep accusing me of killing people?"

He said, "It was just a hunch. You're surely not going to tell me you wanted to knock me out so's you could have your wicked way with my fair white body, I hope."

She laughed weakly and confessed, "I was promised three hundred for your body, in shape to wake up by the

126

time you were well out to sea. Bunco Kelly, up Portland way, recently delivered some able-bodied seamen he stole from a funeral parlor."

"You were out to shanghai me?" Longarm demanded with an incredulous smile. Then he suddenly let her head flop back to the sloppy rug, and untied her sash and bound her wrists with it across her fully exposed breasts while she kept mumbling he was a sneaky bastard.

Longarm drew the snub-nosed .445 from his boot, and rose to glide over to the door as those footsteps he'd heard on the stairs got ever louder.

There came an odd knock on the door. It had to be a signal. Longarm didn't knock back. He opened the door. The two of them were already running back down the stairs. So he shouted, "Freeze or I'll fire!"

They just kept going, so he fired, and the two of them went ass-over-teakettle down the bottom third of the stairs to wind up in a tangled pile on the landing as Longarm tore down after them.

"She ratted on us!" a familiar voice moaned as the wiry little Doc Farnsworth rolled half off the bigger one lying facedown. Longarm never had time to explain that that rat had been his own grand notion. For the mean-eyed little crook was drawing a derringer of his own from under his blood-soaked frock coat.

So Longarm shot him again, this time just over the left eye, and that extra fraction of an inch Mister Webley added to his ammunition didn't really matter when you put a round there.

Rolling the treacherous traveling salesman off his bigger comrade or follower, Longarm saw that the other one was still breathing. He sure was a healthy cuss. Or he *had* been, before the same .445 round had passed through both their chests from above and behind. It took a healthy man to keep breathing with one lung shattered, full of bone fragments and collapsed like a wrung-out bloody sponge.

Hunkered beside him, Longarm demanded, "What was

the name of the vessel you were fixing to sign me aboard, pard?''

The burly hulk in seaman's denim dungarees and navy-blue pea jacket mumbled, ''Go fuck yourself, cowboy! You'll never get me to peach on my shipmates.''

It would have been unkind to tell him he just had. Longarm had reloaded the Webley and tucked it back in his boot by the time a copper badge came cautiously up the outside steps, his own gun drawn, to call out, ''Somebody in there fired a gun?''

Longarm called back, ''I did. Twice. I'd be U.S. Deputy Marshal Custis Long of the Denver District Court, and we need an ambulance wagon here the day before yesterday. I'm talking about one shot dead, one lung-shot, and another poisoned up the stairs!''

So the police got cracking, and in less than an hour they had the one called Doc over at the municipal morgue and Silken Sally and the mate off the S.S. *Queensland* hand-cuffed to their beds and under police guard at Saint Francis Hospital.

Longarm was naturally asked to give a complete deposition over at City Hall. The nearby mint sent their Treasury Agent Coletti to sit in with the other local, state, and federal agents interested in the case. Longarm and Coletti had worked together earlier on other matters involving the gold standard. So Longarm knew Coletti's facts and figures were safe to accept.

But first he had to tell everyone there how he'd been sent out their way by Billy Vail to work with Marshal Seaforth and so on. It made for tedious telling even when you left the private stuff out. One of the city detectives who knew more about the earlier lives of the lady he identified as Silken Sally Sullivan asked how she'd been in bed.

Longarm smiled sheepishly and truthfully replied, ''I wish I knew. She sure was built. But she never really loved me. She and the one called Doc Farnsworth played it foxy aboard the night boat. I suspect we'll find they struck up conversations with lots of men traveling alone. Most of them were never trifled with, and never knew they'd been considered for a long voyage at piss-poor wages—if they were lucky.''

A portly older cuss in navy white-dress said, ''That tramp steamer has been impounded. Neither her captain nor any member of her crew above the rank of deckhand is going anywhere until we get us some damned answers.''

Longarm suggested, ''Tell 'em that mate the skipper sent with Doc to pipe me aboard has turned state's evidence. That ought to shiver some timbers. He intimated he'd been sworn to silence. But once he'd been identified, the rest wasn't hard to put together. They don't send the mate of a short-handed tramp steamer ashore to pick posies.''

Coletti from Treasury asked if Longarm thought the captain and crew of the S.S. *Queensland* were involved in the killings of those floating Chinese.

Longarm shook his head and said, ''I doubt they know anything about that. You don't get much work out of a dead man when you shanghai him. But try her this way. Doc, Silken Sally, and whoever else they might be working with only stood to make a few hundred on each drifter they sold alive as cheap labor. She told me I was worth three hundred to her. That was likely her cut. I ain't sure what the going rate for a shanghaied apprentice seaman might be.''

The navy man said, ''I am. It's seven-fifty outward-bound. If they haven't shaped up by the time they're homeward-bound, they never get home.''

Longarm grimaced and said, ''That's likely why they have to keep grabbing fresh victims wherever they can. I've been told, and I see no reason to doubt, that it's tough to shanghai drunks off the docks in this port. But Frisco's a busy port and mean skippers have a tough time putting out from Frisco fully manned. So the gang I just tangled with had a ready market, if only they could safely shanghai *some* poor souls. I can't be the first one they scouted and be-friended aboard a night boat, then lured well clear of the water and waterfront before Silken Sally made her simple but effective move. It's too early to say for certain, but I suspect we'll be hearing from at least some of the gang's earlier victims sooner or later. You can shanghai some of the people some of the time, but you can't keep them all from a U.S. consulate on some far shore all of the time.''

The navy man grimly agreed, and promised things were going to go hard on certain ship owners as well as their cutthroat crews.

It wouldn't have been polite to tell him how often anyone rich enough to own a ship wound up in jail. Turning to the Treasury agent, Longarm asked, ''What have you to say about recent raw gold sales, old pal?''

Coletti shrugged and said, ''Not much. I've been paying attention. You're not the first to inquire about Chinese prospectors dragging in a few ounces of color at a time. They don't. We do get a modest but fairly steady amount of placer color from Chinese in business suits who may well be tong officials. Treasury has no stated policy on the tong traditions of the Chinese community.''

A Frisco detective growled, ''We do. But they won't let us run the bastards in, and our only hope is that grand Chinese Exclusion Act we hope Congress will be after passing.''

Another local murmured, ''Oh, I dunno. The tongs have their faults. But they do keep things quiet in Chinatown. Lord knows what the fool Chinks would be up to if they didn't have their own kind policing the lot of them. Lord knows *we* can't get shit out of them after a killing in that jungle!''

Coletti suggested, ''Try her this way. The gang had no use for a dead white man with no real money on him. They had no use for a live Chinese after they'd robbed him of his gold. So they kept the one and threw the others overboard?''

Longarm shook his head and said, ''Try her another way. The other night two different gals almost made a fool of me by pretending to be the same one. It's too long a story to go into, but suffice it to say they had me mighty mixed up as long as I was trying to figure out how the same gal could seem so different at second glance. But once I figured what looked like two different gals had to *be* two different gals, it got very simple.''

Coletti asked, ''Are you saying there could be two gangs of river pirates, one killing prospectors for their gold and another out to shanghai their prey alive?''

Longarm shook his head and said, ''Not now. We've caught the shanghai gang. Sooner or later Silken Sally will help us round up any leftover details, if she knows what's good for her. So that just leaves the one gang stabbing and grabbing aboard the boats, not luring them up on Rincon Hill to slip them knockout drops.''

Coletti groanded, ''Oh, shit, you mean it's only half over?''

To which Longarm could only reply, ''I sure hope so.''

Chapter 17

It had been a long night, and the day wasn't shaping up any shorter by the time Longarm was free to wander some more. They put you through more paperwork out in Frisco than they did in Denver when you had to shoot a couple of jaspers and poison a woman.

It was too late to catch a day boat up to Sacramento, and he'd just have to kill another day at the other end of the line if he held out all day and slept aboard the night boat nobody seemed to be vanishing from. But he had a few Frisco bets to cover, and by then he was getting hungry again. So he went to a certain tearoom where a man could order cold meat pies and hot buttered scones with his tea and enjoy it all in a private booth if he had a mind to. It cost a bit more, but Longarm had a mind to. For the last time he'd enjoyed Miss Ming in a private booth, she'd wanted him to come home with him to her quarters in Chinatown, and he had some other calls to make over yonder, once he caught a few winks.

But once he'd asked the snooty Eurasian hostess with chopsticks in her hair to show him to one of the private booths served by their Miss Ming, the young full-blood Daughter of Han who came in to take his order seemed to be somebody else entirely.

This wouldn't have been a total disaster if Longarm had had more time and wasn't fighting to keep his fool eyes open. The little China doll in a sheath dress of green brocaded silk under a starched white apron was built for the way she wriggled her slim hips as she minced about in those funny felt-soled slippers her kind wore. Her face was mighty fine too. But her English left a lot to be desired. He had to use his hands as well as his lips to order a simple snack, and he didn't ask for anything more complicated than a little grub and a lot of strong tea to perk him up a bit.

She came back in a few minutes with hot buttered toast, some currant jelly, and a pot to serve two cups.

She caught his bemused smile and shook hands with herself under her long green sleeves while asking, "Whassamalla you?"

He said, "Nothing, ma'am. I told you this was what I wanted and this is what you brought me. I was just wondering what happened to the Miss Ming who was working here the last time I stopped by."

She said, "*Me* Missy Ming. Missy Ming Li. Whassamalla me?"

He said, "Not a thing. I was just wondering. Was that other Miss Ming your sister, your cousin, some other kin?"

The girl looked confused, and then decided, "You talkee bow dotta belong to pappa's bluddah?"

Longarm nodded and said, "Cousin. Close enough. Last time I was by, she invited me up to her quarters west of Grant Avenue. I don't reckon you know where that would be, or what I'm talking about, do you?"

She just looked down at him sort of cat-eyed. He'd already figured out that cats weren't really planning to murder you in your sleep when they stared at you that way. Cats stared at everything that way because that was the way their eyes were made. Old boys who weren't used to Oriental eyes were forever revealing diabolical Chinese plots to overthrow the U.S. Government and install their old Dow-

133

ager Empress in the White House, or maybe kidnap all the pretty white girls after they'd stolen all the white men's jobs. Longarm had it on good authority that Chinese worried about some pop-eyed white man on his way home from work suddenly giving in to all that pent-up rage and killing everybody on board a cable car.

He smiled reassuringly and told her not to worry about him anymore. She might have left the booth. She might have just stood there while he ate. But then the floor began to tingle under them, and a crack appeared in the plaster wall across from them as the beaded curtain jingled and Longarm sprang to his feet, shouting, "Earthquake?"

She crashed into him to wrap both arms around him and press him back down as she sobbed what sounded like, "*M'hai!* No go outsidee!"

He just sat back in his chair and allowed her to sit in his lap all she wanted to, as most men would have, until the tremor had passed, if that was what they'd just felt.

He said, "I already knew you weren't supposed to run out in the street during one of them earthquakes Frisco never has, no matter what visitors may feel in their bones."

He poured some tea for her in the extra cup, not wanting to make her feel unwelcome in his lap. "What does *m'hai* mean?" he asked her.

She told him, "*M'hai* mean no in Canton talkee, you savee?"

She delicately sipped some tea as he replied, "I do now. How do you say yes in Cantonese?"

She said, "*Hai* mean yes. . . . cousin say she nebbah say *m'hai* to you?"

Longarm chose his words carefully before he replied, "We seemed to get along tolerable. I taught her to call me Custis, if that means a thing to you, Ming Li."

She blushed under her peach complexion and declared, "Me tell her she not telling tloo when she say you makee hotsee totsee with Melican gul in here an then makeee hotsee totsee belong along *her*?"

134

Longarm smiled sheepishly and allowed he ought to be horsewhipped as a horny rascal. Then, since she was still sitting in his lap, he kissed her, as most men would have.

She kissed back, her accent more French than Cantonese. But as he ran his free hand up her silk sheathed flank Ming Li drew back, set her cup aside, and said, "*M'hai!* Bettah we make hotsee totsee along room belong along me, aftah me get off at sixee!"

He confessed he wasn't ever going to last that long, and explained he'd been up all night and was already starting to feel it a heap.

She told him she'd be back chop-chop, and sprang up to scamper out and let him spread jam on his pastry and eat most of it before she was back with a slip of rice paper folded around a brass key. She kissed him again and said, "You go adless you see on papah an fall down sleepy sleep till me come wakee you up my God *hai*! Cousin say you belly too good fo' missee!"

He allowed her cousin had been too very good to miss too, and he might have kissed her some more then and there. But she didn't want him to. So he went out front, paid off the snooty gal who seemed to feel her shit didn't stink because she was at least half white, and made his way over to the nearest cable car stop.

There was time to buy some fresh three-for-a-nickel cheroots at a newsstand as he waited for a ride. When he mentioned the minor earthquake to the dealer, he got his change with the assurance they never had earthquakes out California way.

The newfangled Frisco cable cars were half the size of the horse-drawn streetcars in Denver and sort of spooky. It looked weird to see a dinky railroad car coming along the rails with neither an iron horse nor a real one pulling it. He knew there was an endless steel cable, miles long, running on rollers under that slot between the tracks. He'd seen diagrams in the *Scientific American* magazine showing how a thingamajig controlled by the brakeman reached down

135

through the slot to grab hold of the cable or let it go, to start or stop. It still felt funny, and woke him up some, to ride the dinky cable car up and then up some more into rarified air for Chinese waitresses. But that other gal at the teahouse had told him she didn't get to go out with many swains of her own kind, and he saw why as he hopped off the cable car at the cross street with its name block-printed on the rice paper in the Roman alphabet.

Thanks to the clear instructions he found the numbered side door to a carriage house with no trouble, and let himself in with the brass key. He went up to a small but nicely furnished layout under the sloping roof. If there were horses stabled below or rats to worry about, he didn't smell either, and by this time was so tuckered out he just didn't give a shit.

He'd locked the door down below after him, figuring she'd have all the keys she needed if she made it her habit to invite gents to make themselves at home.

He found the one ample bed made with sateen sheets under a bright red quilt, and he could only hope Ming Li depended mostly on tips for extra luxuries as he undressed with less speed than he might have if she'd been watching and hung his duds neatly. Then he got into bed bare-ass, with the sensual slickness of those fancy sheets inspiring a tingle in his groin he didn't want to study on just yet.

He plumped up one of the pillows and flopped down by broad daylight because that was the way it was outside and he was too tired to worry about it.

He hadn't known how tired he was until he saw how tough it was to wake up from a deep dreamless sleep with an overhead lamp lit to disclose the simple fact that he hadn't been dreaming. Ming Li *was* really stretched out beside him, naked as a jay and smiling like a mean little kid while she, or somebody, seemed to be sucking him as hard as a stick of sixty-percent Hercules about to go off!

That seemed less possible as he woke all the way up to kiss Ming Li's lush lips. So he grabbed her by a firm young

136

breast for some room to peek, and looked down to see that, sure enough, another gal entirely was playing the French horn with chopsticks in her hair.

He wasn't positive until Ming Li said something in Cantonese and shoved that mighty fine head away to cock her own tawny thigh across his waist. Then he saw that the one who'd been sucking him was that snooty hostess from the tearoom. She was swearing at Ming Li in the same lingo, and added in English that it just wasn't fair!

Longarm told her to hold the thought as Ming Li impaled her childishly tight but wild and wet ring-dang-doo on his raging erection. Longarm felt sort of silly as well as mighty erect with that stuck-up-looking Eurasian gal watching them rut, as if she was watching some scientific experiment instead of sitting up in bed stark naked. He reached out to feel both their tits at once, and the hostess calmly asked which felt better.

He laughed, thrust up into Ming Li as he rolled the other gal's nipple between thumb and forefinger, and truthfully replied, "It's hard to say. Which is better, apples or oranges, when both look ripe and sweet? I'm Custis Long, by the way."

She said he could call her Melody. She likely didn't want to give any Chinese name she might have. He said Melody was a pretty name, and she told him to hurry up and satisfy Ming Li so they could talk about it lying down.

By this time the pure Chinese gal from the teahouse was rolling her head around like her neck was busted and yelling in Cantonese. It sounded dirty. Melody told him Ming Li was too excited to know what she was up to on top of him. So Longarm allowed he'd better take charge, and rolled the wild little gal over on her back to spread her smooth thighs wide and long-dong her as she seemed to be begging for mercy, or more.

Melody dropped down to one bare elbow to peer into the opening and closing space between their bellies as she gasped, "Oh, *T'ien*! Just what have we gotten ourselves into? Or should I ask what you mean to put into the two of us! I confess I was willing to go along with three in a bed up here at my place when she asked, but up until now I've been led to believe three in a bed involved two girls and a boy, not two girls and a stallion!''

Then she shyly asked, ''Could you move it in and out more, Custis? It really makes me hot to watch your big wet shaft sliding in and out of another woman!''

Longarm would have obliged her curiosity had not Ming Li suddenly moaned in mingled joy and wonder and pulled him down against her with her arms and legs wrapped like pythons around his heaving flesh as he came in her at the same time.

Melody translated the younger gal's babbling to mean she'd never come that hard with any mere man before.

Longarm had to allow he'd had worse lays in his day, and he was still recovering from Ming Li, hence feeling more conversational, as he rolled off the one gal to shove the other backwards across the bed, casually asking, ''Does that mean you two play other games up here when I might not be around?''

The bigger and more rounded Eurasian gasped, ''Wait a minute! What are you doing? Give me a chance to get used to the idea. You were just this minute humping Ming Li like a maniac and . . . Oooh! You're so big and I'm so tense and . . . Be gentle, won't you?''

Longarm had no choice at first. He was still winded and half spent from Ming Li as he shoved it slow but steady to Melody, and it might not have been as easy to keep hard if she hadn't started moving her wider hips less wildly but more skillfully than her little pal while she closed her eyes and crooned, ''Forget what I just said! I want it in me big and wet and all the way in and out with every savage thrust!''

He allowed she sure had a poetic way with words as he tried to follow her instructions to the letter. By this time little Ming Li had sat up to watch, and Lord only knows

138

what she was saying as she chattered at them in Cantonese and played with Longarm's balls while he long-donged her older pal and likely mentor.

Longarm braced an elbow under each of Melody's bent knees, and spread his own legs as well for better purchase as he rotated his bare rump to literally screw in and out of her. Then he had to laugh and beg Melody to tell Ming Li in their own lingo to quit trying to shove a finger up his ass.

She told him not to say he didn't like something before he'd tried it. He said he wiped his own ass all the time and didn't have two-inch fingernails, dad blast it! So Melody said something in Cantonese to Ming Li, and she commenced to lick around like a horny pup back there instead, and that felt more silly than scary.

Melody pouted. "What are you laughing about? Do you find us slant-eyed sluts amusing?"

He kissed her soothingly and assured her, "I sure hope you're having half as much fun with my old organ-grinder. But the gals I'm laughing at were two other gals completely. It's too long a story to go into, and I don't like to kiss and tell in any case. But I just got to thinking how simple it might have been for those other gals to come right out and say they wanted to play three in a bed with the lamp lit."

She dug her nails into Longarm's back as she thoughtfully inquired, "Oh? And were those white girls better than Ming Li and me?"

He got to moving in her with renewed inspiration as he truthfully replied, "Not better. Not worse. Different. And thinking about how wild the *five* of us would look in bed if they were here makes me feel horny as all get-out. So Powder River and let her buck!"

Chapter 18

So a good time was had by all, and later he got to know the two of them in a less Biblical sense as the three of them shared a three-for-a-nickel smoke with him sandwiched between their naked cuddles.

The most the gals had in common, aside from being sex maniacs of at least part Chinese ancestry and with the same place of employment, was that they were both outcasts from the Frisco Chinese community.

Ming Li had come to America as a ''picture bride'' with her passage paid by a rich old Chinese who was looking to marry up with anybody that young and pretty.

Ming Li had taken one look at the old fart and run off crying. So the groom-to-be, the marriage broker, and their tong were sort of vexed with the willful little thing.

When he expressed concern, Melody explained, better than Ming Li could have in her pidgin English, how the tongs seldom bothered with sending their *bu how day* after sissy gals. Folks who didn't follow the Chinese drift had the tongs down as crooked gangs. But there was more to the tradition than that. Melody suggested he think of the James-Younger gang as a Chinese highbinder society and Blind Boss Buckley's Frisco machine as a tong. Tongs cut pesky legal corners about as often as a white political machine. But they'd also see about getting you a good job while you were in the Golden Mountain, defend you from outsiders, or just look out for you in exchange for you playing by their rules. They expected a healthy cut of any good fortune you came by with their advice and consent. But despite what some of the California newspapers said about them, the tongs didn't force you to join up. They figured if you didn't want to pay you didn't want to play and you were on your own, an ocean away from your own kith and kin, if and when real crooks of any race moved in on you.

Working in a tearoom, neither tongless gal had much to fear from highbinders or road agents. But Melody said she'd advised Ming Li to pay off that marriage broker if it took her ten years because there was a lot to be said for having a tong to call one's own.

Melody had been left standing behind the door when tong memberships were being passed out because her daddy had been a forty-niner of High Dutch ancestry and her momma had been no better than she should have been, an outcast from the Hip Sings who'd run away from the whorehouse run by a Hip Sing in better standing. Melody said that, like Ming Li, she was in no danger from any hatchet men because killing women for little fun or profit just wasn't their style. She'd grown up understanding how little an outcast Oriental had to fall back on in the American West. Her Chinese mother's white boyfriend, one of the many ''uncles'' who'd come after her white father, had taught her to suck at six and how to fuck, and enjoy it, by the time she was nine. Her mother had thought it was about time she started contributing to her own upkeep. So Melody had, until she was old enough to pass for twelve and ran off with a nice young Chinese for a while.

She shyly confessed that once she'd gotten used to big old hairy-chested ruffians who reminded her of her dear old dad, it was tougher to enjoy life with a boy almost as slender and hairless as herself.

Longarm shut her off with an indelicate grab before she could tell him more than he really wanted to know about other gents she'd known in the Biblical sense. She'd told him enough that really interested a man who could barely find the shithouse in a chop suey joint.

The fact that there were Chinese, lots of Chinese, who were no longer part of the original tight-knit bunch was something to study on. He'd read somewhere that there'd been around thirty thousand Chinese in the country by the end of the California gold rush. There were now around a hundred and thirty thousand, as that rabble-rouser Denis Kearney never got tired of warning, and whether you pictured them all plotting to assassinate President Hayes and make the First Lady an opium-crazed white slave or not, that was still one hell of a lot of Chinese. So if only one out of a hundred took to cutting his pigtail off and acting as independent as these two mighty independent little things, you still had thirteen hundred or so Sons of Han who could be up to almost anything without more traditional Chinese such as Little Pete ever hearing about it.

He passed the cheroot to Ming Li, and asked Melody how a white man might go about having a friendly meeting with somebody higher up in a tong than a hatchet man in his teens.

She said, "Ask me directions to the end of the rainbow and I'll give it a try. If another *Chinese* asked directions to any tong in Chinatown, he would be met by blank stares and asked what a tong was. People who have business with tong leaders know how to find them. If the leaders have business with anybody, they will be shown to a door in an alley that might or might not be a tong headquarters."

He said in that case he'd settle for some lessons in Cantonese. She gave him a French lesson instead, and after he'd screwed them both again, Melody explained how silly that request had been while little Ming Li whipped them up a wok of *lo mein*. Melody explained *lo* meant pork when it didn't mean gong. She used the example of how the English

142

sound spelled "to," "too," or "two," and said Cantonese had far more different meanings for every ding, dong, or dell in the lingo, depending on how they were said—or actually, sung. But she allowed he was on the money when he made an educated guess that *mein* had to mean noodles on that particular occasion.

Ming Li wanted to get on top while she fed him with chopsticks.

Then it was Melody's turn again.

But he managed to catch a few winks between times, and thanks to the unbroken nap he'd had before the gals got off from work, Longarm woke up the next morning bright-eyed if not bushy-tailed, and they had to have mercy on him because it was time for them to go back to work.

Having learned about as much Cantonese as he was likely to at the Frisco end of the river run, Longarm elected to catch the earlier of the day boats heading up to Sacramento. He didn't board it to go to Sacramento. He aimed to stop off at Reedport, gather together his old saddle and Winchester, and board the later day boat with them when it stopped there.

He was starting to feel that, as tedious a town as it was next to Frisco, the state capital, closer to the gold fields, might be a better hunting ground.

The river pirates who'd been stabbing and grabbing aboard the night boats had been too slick by half to be choosing their victims by guess and by golly. With everybody from Marshal Seaforth and his deputies to Little Pete and his hatchet men watching for them, they'd been getting away with it, slow but steady. Longarm suspected they had to be choosing their victims well in advance, before they ever got on any boat.

He said so, standing at the bar in the main salon with a purser who had to know who he really was because the purser of a passenger vessel was charged with keeping law and order on board as well as an eye on the baggage. So a lawman working in secret without the purser in on it would

143

be in the same awkward spot as an outside lawman pussy-footing around a trail town without telling the town law. It could smart to be shot in the ass by another lawman who thought you were a hired gun after one of his own wayward youths.

As they sipped morning pick-me-ups with nobody else listening, the purser confided he'd tried more than once to warn one of those victims. A nice old Chinese gent called Chang had vanished over the side with or without his poke. The purser said advising the heathens to check their pokes with him for safekeeping was sort of like singing tenor in a Pacific typhoon. Nobody tried to stop you, but nobody heard you, no matter how loud you sang.

He added, "The poor benighted bastards *know* somebody has been stabbing and robbing prospectors down from the hills, and they've still refused to let us help them guard their gold. I don't know what makes them so stubborn, do you?"

Longarm drank a shandy of lemonade and lager and replied, "Us. Not all of us, but enough of us to make the Sons of Han sort of shy about entrusting us with their hard-earned color. It was before my time, but I understand that during the big gold rush it was considered sort of comical to let a Chinese bust his back prospecting and then jump his claim as soon as he got to producing. Like many a white prospector, a lot of Chinese with neither the luck nor literary skills to file on any claim have spent considerable time panning tailings, only to have ruthless whites in days of yore or more recent days rob the poor cusses."

The purser said, "Tailings? I'm afraid I'm more of a seafaring man than a mining engineer, Deputy Long."

Longarm explained, "Tailings are what's left after you've crushed ore and run it through your sluice box, mercury table, or whatever to extract most of the color. I say *most,* not *all,* because the bigger mine operators have to worry about diminishing returns. A hardrock miner worth paying is going to take home three dollars every shift whether he produces three dollars worth of pay dirt or not. If the ore's high-grade, it's easy enough for him to earn his keep running the crushed ore through once or twice and just chucking the processed tailings aside, so you can process some more high-grade, see?''

The purser brightened and said, ''Sure. You're saying somebody with more time, willing to pan less than three dollars worth of color a shift, could just poke around old played-out mines and swish crushed ore from the sort of trash piles around in a pan with some water till he saw some color.''

Longarm said, ''That's about the size of it. Lots of old sourdoughs fall back on panning tailings between serious hunts for El Dorado. It ain't no path to sudden wealth. But on the other hand, you know when you squat down by a tailings pile that there must have been *some* color in the dirt to begin with or there wouldn't be such a pile left over.''

The purser grimaced and said, ''Well, every man to his own taste, and I reckon it's tougher for a Chinaman to get a job as a dollar-a-day cowhand. But I'd still like to see somebody hang for stabbing them and grabbing such hard-earned booty. How much do you figure they've been making on an average victim?''

Longarm said, ''I doubt they've been choosing average victims. I was told by a Chinese who ought to know that few of the Sons of Han coming down the river could have more than a hundred or so in their pokes. But you're right about it taking a lot of panning to gather that much most of the time.''

He sipped more of the shandy and continued. ''I suspect somebody has been scouting them up Sacramento way, before they ever got on the boat. For whether a man pokes through old tailings, or tries his luck along a creek bed that ain't been worked for a while, his efforts can pan out for richer or poorer. Most of the color anyone pans in a virgin placer is literal gold dust. You wind up with a small glob of heavier glitter as you swish lighter sand and silt around and around and around. But now and again you find a nugget in your pan, from the size of a bigger grain of sand up to a sort of gilded raisin, or even a prune. Just a few such finds could make a man richer than he ever expected to wind up gleaning through the old gold fields.''

The purser said if he ever found a gold nugget the size of a prune, he wouldn't talk to strangers about it.

Longarm nodded soberly and said, ''I doubt anybody has. A heap of 'em don't speak English. But I just last night learned how many Chinese there are who ain't connected with any clan, tong, or whatever and feel less call to play by the usual rules. I suspect we're looking for some two-face more than one Chinese prospector has trusted literally with his life.''

The purser marveled, ''Jesus, who might that be?''

Longarm shrugged and said, ''Can't say. The infernal Chinese *won't* say, even when we *ask* them.''

The purser finished his own drink and got back to riding herd on the day passengers and their baggage. Longarm had no baggage with him. So he went out on deck and smoked at the port rail until the day boat stopped at Reedport and let him off along with a piano and some fancy whorehouse mirrors from Venice, Italy.

Longarm didn't investigate where such luxuries might be headed. He walked up to the Widow Seaforth's house, and found the copper-headed Mairi sort of red-eyed when she met him at the door with a gallant smile.

He didn't ask why at first. She assured him his saddle, Winchester, and .44-40 were upstairs where he'd left them, and invited him back to her kitchen for some coffee and a sort of cherry pie made with grapes. California folks sure cooked strangely.

He told her he had time for seconds before that next steamer came along, and for some reason that got her to watering her apron with her eyes as she fought hard not to bawl out loud.

Longarm set his coffee mug aside and rose to stride around to her side of the table and just hold her against his vest as he quietly told her, "I can't do nothing about it if you won't tell me what it is, Miss Mairi."

She buried her face in rough tobacco-brown tweed and sobbed that there was nothing he *could* do, seeing he had that other boat to catch.

He said, "There will always come another boat, Miss Mairi. What's wrong? Has somebody been messing with you?"

She laughed bitterly and said, "That will be the day as long as Miwok Mason keeps warning one and all that I'm his chosen true love! They're holding a church social up the post road next week, and Miwok is the only one who's offered to take me. Nobody else would dare. So I guess I'll just have to stay home and miss the fun again."

Longarm said, "No, you won't," and let go of her to march out of the kitchen and up the stairs. He came right back down without his frock coat on. As Mairi regarded him standing there in his vest and shirt sleeves, she quietly asked, "Custis, why have you strapped on your gun again? Uncle Tavish said you were working in secret to catch those river pirates."

Longarm grimly replied, "I am. But I ain't after river pirates at the moment."

Chapter 19

Thanks to thirty-odd miles on the day boat and the time it had taken to get the sad story out of Mairi Seaforth, it was well after noon when Longarm stepped out of bright sunlight into the beer-and-tobacco-scented gloom of the one saloon in town. There were only a few early drinkers. A little red-nosed barfly who wanted to be everybody's pal told him Miwok Mason generally rode in with his Mexicans before supper time, even though nobody in town had ever invited him to supper.

Longarm dryly remarked that hope sprang eternal, and stepped back out into the glare. That was where Mairi Seaforth caught up with him, since she'd found it impossible to follow a man into a saloon.

As Longarm ticked his hat brim to her, Mairi said, "Custis, I can handle Miwok, and I won't have you fighting him for my sake."

Longarm said, "Ain't aiming to for your sake alone, no offense. The other evening he came close to killing and surely disfigured a harmless farm boy for life. They say he did it to warn others not to even think about calling on a certain handsome widow woman."

She said, "I heard about that. I mean to give Miwok a piece of my mind about his mean ways the next time he comes courting, the silly brute. But to tell the truth, Miwok may only be part of my problem here in Reedport.''

Longarm nodded soberly and said, "You can only eat an apple a bite at a time and solve a problem a part at a time, Miss Mairi. When I see a lit fuse attached to a powder keg, I feel I'd better snuff it out. We had born bullies like Miwok going to school with us, back before any of us were packing guns. Most born bullies learn to control their mean natures in grammar school. It only takes a bloody nose and a few black eyes to improve their manners if they have a lick of sense. But now and again a kid's too stupid, or too sheltered by rich kin, to get over such a thing naturally. I have to go talk to some other folks now, Miss Mairi. Why don't you just run along and let me worry about this business?''

She stamped a foot in the dust and insisted, "It's not your business! You're a federal lawman, not a moon calf out to carry me off to a church social! I've talked to Uncle Tavish about Miwok's crazy notion that I'm his true love. Uncle Tavish says there's nothing he can do about it as long as Miwok doesn't do something personal to a kinswoman. He says he can't lower himself to interfere in public brawls between local ruffians. That's all Miwok is, a ruffian!''

Longarm said, "Your uncle may be right as far as the dignity of his own office is concerned. My home office is far away, and I don't much care what they say about me as long as it ain't no lie.''

He stepped around her, seeing she wouldn't budge, and strode on across the way to the combined corral, livery, and smithy run by a burly Mex *herrero*.

He was glad to see Mairi headed somewhere else as he joined the beefier and somewhat older *herrero* under the overhang of his forge.

A Mexican in his teens was pumping the bellows while some little kids supervised. The *herrero* murmured in Spanish, and the kid rested on the long handle of the bellows

149

as the boss in the leather apron shoved the horseshoe he'd been hammering back in the forge, but hung on to the hammer and tongs as he quietly asked Longarm what he wanted.

Longarm said he was looking for a pal from Old Mexico who'd been spotted up this way. He was lying, of course, when he added, "He shot a *rurale* down in Nogales and you know how picky *los rurales* can be. I wanted to head him off before he gets into trouble up this way, seeing he's never been this far north."

The *herrero* complimented Longarm on the way he pronounced those few words of Spanish, and added, *"Habla 'spañol, Señor?"*

Longarm smiled modestly and replied, *"Poquito.* I've been trying to learn Chinese too. But your English is way better than my Spanish or even Chinese. I'm a lawman name of Custis Long, but I have warrants on this old Mexican boy, who's only crime is that he can't abide that cocksucking El Presidente Diaz south of the border."

The *herrero* cautiously said, "We see few of *La Raza* who might not have been born up this way. Does your rebel friend have a name?"

Longarm placed one finger alongside his nose, winked, and confided, "Riders like him don't freely state their true names and addresses. We just call him El Gato."

The older man's jaw dropped. Then he suddenly beamed and declared, "I know who you are. You are the *gringo muy simpático* my people know as El Brazo Largo, The Long Arm! Where are you staying here in Reedport? Is there anything you need? Is there anything we can get you? Would you like to meet some nice girls?"

Longarm smiled fondly and replied, "I wish I had time. I won't be here long enough to take you up on such kind offers. If my pal don't show up, I'll be moving on as soon as I settle a score with the bully of your town. I think they call him Miwok. Whatever they call him, I have a bone to pick with him about *another* pal he's been pestering."

The Mexican's face went wooden as he quietly suggested, "I would not pick bones with that one if I were you, El Brazo Largo. It would not be difficult for a man of your reputation to swat him like a fly. But he has real men, of *La Raza,* riding for him."

Longarm shrugged and said, "Thanks for warning me. Should El Gato turn up looking for me, would you tell him I'll be over to the one saloon?"

The *herrero* insisted, "I would bet upon you and El Gato against a cavalry troop, El Brazo Largo. But El Gato is not here yet, and those hombres riding with Miwok Mason are *muy malo y muy pronto*!"

Longarm allowed he'd just have to be a tad meaner and faster in that case, and headed back to the saloon. He knew his advertising would spread like wildfire among the Mexicans born north of the border as U.S. citizens. That had been his purpose in advertising, although there were less misleading statements printed on the labels of many a patent medicine.

Seeing how early it still seemed, Longarm bought a deck of cards and some extra smokes off the barkeep along with a pitcher of beer and a bowl of peanuts. Then he took them all over to a corner table and set things up conveniently. Then he drew his six-gun and set it on the table before he sat down with his back in the corner.

Somebody muttered, "Jeeesus!" and a couple of regulars left as Longarm commenced to deal solitaire to help him nurse his peanuts and suds. But some of them stayed, as some usually did, and some others came in as news spread fast in a town that size. Most of them took up positions well out of the line of fire between Longarm's chosen corner and the bat-wing doorway. But the same little barfly with the coyote grin from before came over to warn, "Some of the boys say you're out to arrest somebody, Deputy Long. We didn't know we had any outlaws here in Reedport."

Longarm turned over a card, trumped it, and quietly said,

"The son of a bitch I'm after ain't here yet. That's how come I'm playing cards with myself instead of cleaning his plow."

The little barfly left. Longarm wasn't surprised a few minutes later when a bigger squirt came in wearing a pewter badge and a Starr .36. He came over, pulled a chair up from another table, and sat down to say without preamble, "Allow me to introduce myself. I am Franklin Jefferson Beckworth, the town marshal, and I don't like to see trouble here in Reedport."

Longarm said, "I noticed. You didn't do shit when Miwok Mason beat the hell out of that kid the other night."

Beckworth blustered, "That was a personal fair fight I had no call to take sides in."

Longarm smiled thinly and said, "Don't take sides in this one then. I mean it. Don't you have a sandbox somewhere else to play in?"

Beckworth blustered, "You can't talk to me like that! I'm the law!"

To which Longarm simply replied, "No, you ain't. You're either a lazy bum or a coward wearing a badge you ain't been backing up worth shit. A lawman is by definition a man who upholds the law. Are you saying it's lawful to beat a man to a pulp while your riders hold him for you?"

Beckworth said, "I'm going to wire your boss, Marshal Seaforth, and tell him you've gone crazy."

He must have meant to. He left. Longarm went on dealing solitaire, eating peanuts one at a time, and nursing his pitcher as the suds went flat for what sure seemed a tedious time. Then somebody stuck in his head to yell, "They're riding in!" and dashed out to find some cover.

Longarm ground out the cheroot he'd been smoking as he heard hoofbeats and the sounds of men reining in and dismounting across the way at the *herrero*'s corral. He still managed to deal himself a whole new hand by the time Miwok Mason swaggered through the bat wings in all his bearded buckskinned glory.

The bully was alone as he caught sight of Longarm in the corner and demanded, "What have you been saying about me to them Mexicans? My *vaqueros* just quit on me! All three of them! I don't savvy the lingo well enough to follow what you told that old Mex blacksmith."

As everyone else in the place seemed to hold his breath, Longarm easily replied, "Nothing that wasn't the pure truth. I simply declared you were a chickenshit yellow-livered cur dog. I never said you were a mother-fucker because I doubt you'd have the nerve to fuck a grown woman. Pissants like you go to dances and start fights so they don't have to ask any gal to dance."

It got very quiet in there as all the color seemed to drain from Miwok Mason's usually florid face. Then somebody snickered, and Miwok came unstuck to demand, "Are you trying to provoke a fight with me?"

Longarm wasn't the only one in there who laughed. But he was the one who said, "Why, no. I was hoping you'd crawl under this table and suck my dick. Tell me something, Miwok, did you ever take it in your mouth to make money?"

That one little barfly volunteered from a safe distance, "If any man ever spoke to me that way and I was packing two guns, I'd surely be slapping leather by this time!"

Miwok stared in horror at the .44-40 on the table between Longarm and himself. Then he tried, "You're known to be a gunslick, and you've already helped yourself to an edge on me. It ain't fair to insult a man when you have an edge on him!"

Longarm slowly rose to his considerable height, picked up his side arm, and put it back in its holster on his left hip, then quietly asked, "Is that better for you, cock-sucker?"

As others laughed more openly now, Miwok stared wildly around to plead, "Can't any of you see what he's doing? He's trying to get me to draw so he can kill me!

He figures I either have to take such shit from him or draw!''

A disgusted voice from the crowd inquired, "Then why don't you go ahead and *draw,* Miwok?"

Another jeered, "Ain't you supposed to be the fastest gun in the Big Valley, Miwok?"

The fastest gun in the Big Valley desperately unbuckled his gunbelt and let it fall to the sawdust-covered floor as he sobbed, "It ain't right! This is my town! You boys ain't supposed to root for anybody from other parts!"

Then he almost sobbed at Longarm, "You can see I ain't armed, and if you shoot me in the back I'll charge you with cold-blooded murder!"

Then he turned his back on Longarm and tore out the door, bawling about getting even with them all.

Everybody wanted to buy Longarm a drink after that. Longarm said he still had a lot of suds left and moved the pitcher, cards, and such to another table closer to the front and across the doorway from the bar. The barkeep was the first one to see why. He rolled his eyes up at the pressed-tin ceiling and announced, "Last round, gents. We're closing early this evening."

Somebody protested that the sun hadn't set outside yet. The barkeep said he had to take inventory as he cast an edgy glance at Longarm across the way. Longarm just went on dealing solitaire. He'd put his six-gun atop his new table, as before. There was no law saying a saloon couldn't close for the night before sundown. But he had no call to leave before they asked him to.

The barkeep might have. Some of the others finished their last suds and filed out. Others nursed their drinks at the bar or anywhere out of the likely lines of fire. Waiting to see what came next.

What came next was Miwok Mason at a dead run from across the street with his saddle gun, a .50-caliber Spencer repeater, leading the way with its muzzle as he busted

154

through the bat wings, blazing away at where Longarm had been seated earlier.

Miwok pumped four rounds at the empty chair behind the vacated table before he saw he wasn't shooting at anybody in the dim light. He still had three rounds in the Spencer's tubular magazine. So Longarm fired thrice from his new position, aiming low because he was in trouble if the rascal died.

One two-hundred-grain .44 ball propelled by forty grains of powder sliced Miwok's ass open across both buttocks. One round hit him just below his hip joint, shattered his femur, and tickled his balls to go on into his other thigh and damage it considerably. Another round missed completely. Longarm was only human. But the two that scored left Miwok on the sawdust, bawling like a baby, until somebody fetched that same doc who'd ridden down to Frisco with that other banged-up boy. He'd just come back in time, the doc chortled, to see the devil get his due.

The sun had set by the time they'd patched Miwok up enough to take his own boat ride down to the hospital in Frisco. The doc said he needed some time there before he'd ever walk again, with a limp.

There was no sense waiting with a gunshot victim by the river until the nightboat came along way later. So nobody noticed Marshal Seaforth getting out of his own launch tied up at the pier before he'd joined the crowd in the saloon, which hadn't closed after all.

Longarm turned from the bar to greet him, saying, "Howdy, Marshal. I reckon they've told you about some excitement we just had here?"

Tavish Seaforth stared stony-eyed at Longarm and replied in an icy tone, "They have. You're off the case. I never asked Billy Vail to send me a homicidal maniac. I'll be staying here to tidy up the mess you've just made. My launch is tied up at the pier with a head of steam. Tell the boys who run it which way you want them to take you, and get the hell out of my sight before we have another shootout here tonight!''

Longarm started to say something else, shrugged, and said, ''Billy Vail told me you'd be in command. So *adios*, and ain't it amazing I ain't at all surprised to see you so pissed off at me.''

Chapter 20

The deputies manning the steam launch never said what their boss might have told them about Longarm. He must have told them *something,* because nobody wanted to talk to him, and he got to ride up in the bows alone with his baggage. Reedport was less than halfway up to Sacramento, so the long night ride would have felt more lonesome if Longarm had let it. But some wise old philosopher had advised younger men to never pass up a chance to take a piss or catch forty winks. So Longarm pissed over the side in the dark, and spread the bedroll from his McClellan on the duckboards ahead of the upright boiler. But he left his boots on and dozed with his six-gun under the rolled-up frock coat he used as a pillow.

They dropped him on the Sacramento quay in the wee small hours. He told them he loved them too, and toted his load to a dinky hotel across from the steam line's slips. He wasn't all that tired now. He needed a new base to work out of where his possibles would be safe. He was vexed as all get-out with himself for hauling a saddle and bridle all the way to the coast to ride steamboats. But that was the trouble with not knowing how to read your future before you caught up with it.

He found a waterfront beanery, and had fried eggs over

chili con carne with some black coffee to get himself going as the sun rose over the snowy peaks to the east. It was still too early to do anything else. He knew he was supposed to wire home and tell Billy Vail he'd been fired.

On the other hand he somehow doubted Marshal Seaforth intended to wire an old pal and tell him he had a hard-on for a niece by marriage. So Longarm figured he had at least the coming weekend to work with, and it pissed him considerably that he'd been asked to head back to Denver with not one of those murders of Chinese prospectors aboard the night boats solved.

Nothing much was open in Sacramento yet as Longarm strolled the downtown streets that were just starting to come to life.

He paused by a plate-glass window to admire all the Chinese shit they had on display. He couldn't tell what sort of folks ran the place. Lots of regular Americans liked to buy Oriental curios, and some of the small heathen notions were curious as hell. They had a whole pantheon of odd-looking deities lined up on one rosewood bench, carved out of ivory or what looked like the briar root you made expensive tobacco pipes out of.

As he was standing there a familiar voice asked, "Had enough of that Sweet Jesus joss, Foreign Devil?"

Longarm turned to smile down at Little Pete the hatchet man and explain, "I ain't as certain as some who's right or wrong."

Little Pete said, "Neither am I. My people follow three religions at the same time, and I can't buy into any of 'em. My elders used to pray to some of those *Kuans* in the back row. This shop sells a sort of limited collection of the popular ones. Lots of your women seem to buy a statue of Kuan Yin there. She's the serene-looking lady who keeps gals out of other trouble and helps them have kids if they want 'em."

Longarm smiled at the pretty little figure on the other side of the glass and said, "I know about Kuan Yin. A more religious Chinese told me all about her offering her place in heaven to a poor doomed sinner and being turned into a goddess by Buddha. The Navaho know her as Changing Woman. Some say all the nations that speak Na-Déné came out of Asia a spell later than other Indians.''

Little Pete shrugged and said, ''That story about her having mercy on somebody like me is only one version. Like I said, my people have a whole shithouse of beliefs and never see any contradiction. That's why we sell so many lottery tickets every year. When *you* guys get new gods you kill everybody who believes in the older ones. My people kept all their old-time nature gods when they bought the Buddha, kept *him* in all his confusing shapes when they went with The Way, and don't ask me to even try and explain Taoism. If I was going to buy any of it I guess I would go with Kung Fu Tse. You people call him Confucius. Picture Christ without the miracles. Just the good advice.''

Longarm said, ''I read some of his sayings. It's tough to argue with a man who states the obvious. Who's that really big ivory cuss in the funny hat, Pete?''

The agnostic hatchet man said, ''Oh, that's old Yu Huang Shang Ti or just Yu Ti. He's the big cheese in *T'ien,* or what you'd call Heaven.''

Longarm asked, ''Can't you make up your mind what to call such an important god?''

Little Pete demanded, ''Can't you guys say Jesus Christ or Lord as the spirit moves you? Yu Huang Shang Ti means August Personage of the Jade Emperor. Yu Ti just means Jade Personage. There's nobody else it *could* mean when you use Lord for Jesus, and it works the same for us, see?''

Longarm allowed he reckoned so, and asked if the hatchet man and his cutthroat crew meant to catch the same night boat down to Frisco. Little Pete pointed out that nobody he gave a shit about had ever been murdered on any *other* river run. So Longarm said they'd talk about that later, adding, ''I ain't sure my boss would want me to make

159

one more run if I told him I was fixing to. So I'd best just join you aboard the damn boat and not pester my home office about it.''

They shook on that and parted friendly. By then Sacramento had come to life. So Longarm proceeded to run himself ragged as he discovered how swell notions could pan out more complicated than expected.

He found his way to the nearest public library and flashed his badge at a vapidly pretty and right sunny library gal who said she'd be proud to show him their best set of encyclopedias. He found what he thought he was after, took some notes, and left the library to ask directions to the state bureau of mines and mineral claims, where he got to talk to an ugly old cuss who seemed gloomy as all get-out.

But they got along tolerably, once Longarm explained who he was and what he was looking for. The older man said he'd been there during the big gold rush, and agreed that abandoned placer claims were the ones Longarm ought to dig out of the files because the bigger deep-shaft operators ran everything they dug out of the ground through stamping mills that reduced everything to grit that could pass through a flour sifter.

The old-timer also agreed that Chinese gleaning abandoned placers with their gold pans would feel safer in some parts of the old gold fields than others. Then he shot a big hole in Longarm's grand notion when he pointed out that nobody had found one speck of nephrite, which was the fancy term for jade, anywhere in the Sierra Nevada in living memory.

So Longarm went back to the library, and that pretty gal seemed so glad to see him she brought him a whole stack of tomes. That was what you called books almost too heavy to lift. Tomes.

It was a musty, dusty chore old Henry back at the Denver office might have enjoyed more. But Longarm made more notes about China and Chinese notions than he'd ever thought a white man might need, and told the gal she'd been a big help to the U.S. Justice Department.

She allowed that made her feel proud, and asked if he'd care to walk her home when they closed and tell her folks about it while they all had supper together.

She looked mighty chagrined when Longarm said that reminded him he had to pick up his kids at his mother-in-law's before supper time. He hadn't wanted her to think he didn't think she was worth courting.

He had time for some needled beer and cold cuts before he met up with Little Pete along the riverside again. He handed the baby-faced killer the notebook pages he'd torn out and said, "I want you to read this list of gold camps and tell me which of the Chinese prospectors who were robbed and killed might have worked old played-out placers close enough to matter."

Little Pete glanced at the short list Longarm had made over at the mine and claims bureau, made a wry face, and said, "Just guessing without checking, I'd say *all* of them. Our guys get along a lot better with the Anglos and Mexicans south of the American River, where most of these old camps seem to lie. So what's the big secret? We've known all along the robbery victims had been reworking old placers up in the gold fields."

"We have, and we thought they'd been panning *gold,*" Longarm replied. As the young hatchet man stared blankly at him, he explained. "I've just found out a heap of stuff I never knew about two or three related rocks valued higher than gold in China. *We* call it *jade*. Most of the finest so-called Chinese jade comes from Burma or Turkestan. You Sons of Han have always bought and cherished it as a rare foreign import!"

The young Chinese said, "I thought you were going to tell me something I didn't know. Old-timers in Chinatown are crazy about the stuff. They collect it as carvings. They carry smooth chunks of jade around just to feel up, like a spare dick, and families go in hock to buy a lump of jade to put in a dead relative's mouth for a proper burial. I like the look and feel of the shit myself. What about it?''

Longarm said, "The forty-niners didn't know what you just told me. Those few who might have bothered to ask would have been told those green rocks and pebbles you find in some watersheds, but only some, were *jadeite*, not the true *nephrite* jade of Far Cathay. So whether they knew what it was or not, they tended to toss it aside as they panned for gold. Most of what they dug out of the creek beds, heavier than regular granite and such, would still be around the edges of abandoned workings to be found.''

Longarm nodded at the list he'd handed the kid as he went on. "I just found out Chinese jade merchants make no great distinction betwixt Old World nephrite and New World jadeite. Both are silicates formed in hot springs, and you have to be a chemist to tell much difference. To the extent they ain't the same, the American jadeite, or shit-that-seems-to-be-jade in chemistry talk, is a tad heavier, harder, and holds a better shine than the old-time jade your kind has always been willing to pay so much for. Let's talk about how much. I understand a select piece of high-quality jade can go for three to five times its weight in gold. Are you with me so far?''

Little Pete nodded grimly and said, "It ain't nice to hold out on the tong that's grubstaked you for a prospecting trip! What do you call one of your own miners when they pocket hunks of really high-grade ore in a hardrock mine?''

Longarm said, "High-graders. Mine owners who don't belong to any tong have been known to string high-graders up with few formalities.''

Little Pete said, "*Hai!* Misguided men carrying secret caches of jade they never told us about changes the picture completely! You're wrong about prize jade being worth five times its weight in gold. I told you lots of rich old farts don't care *what* they have to pay for the really *good* stuff. One of our boys holding out on his tong would never try to sneak anything *less* down the river. We're talking about a serious breach of tong traditions here. The risk just wouldn't be worth it unless a boy working an old placer alone took his time and selected nothing but prime specimens."

Longarm said, "I'm glad to see we see it about the same way. Not that anyone as upright and square as yourself would dream of it, of course, but how would you go about fencing prize jade without your tong hearing about it? I somehow can't see going to Fong the jeweler with a lump of raw jadeite. Can you?"

Little Pete shook his head and said, "They say confession is good for the soul, but I'm not about to tell a lawman the details of the terrible risk those boys were taking. In a way it's just as well for them they were only stabbed and thrown overboard. They had to be working for or with outcast Cantonese, or your own breed of fence. Once the chain of ownership had been reshuffled, it would be easy enough for a Frisco import-export outfit to put the stuff on the Chinese market."

Longarm said, "I was afraid you'd say that. It's a whole new ball game with a change of teams. A secretly rich Chinese sleeping on the cargo deck with a king's ransom in jade instead of a gold poke hidden on him makes it a game any number might want to play!"

Little Pete grimaced and said, "Not tonight, Josephine. My boys and me will be watching all the round-eyed devils traveling second-class."

He brightened as he waved the short list and added, "Thanks to this tip we won't have to keep an eye on *all* our boys. Just the ones who've been reworking old claims around these particular camps!"

Longarm asked how sure Little Pete and his hatchet men might feel about where a particular Son of Han might have been poking about for low-grade placer color. He dryly added, "A man who'd fib about a pretty green rock in his duffle might not want to say just where he's been wandering in the high country of late."

Little Pete shook his head and said, "Too risky. Our

163

boys stand out like sore thumbs where your boys are friendly. So a Cantonese buying so much as a twist of tobacco at a crossroads general store would be taking too big a chance if he said he'd been far away from it that day. When one of us comes across one of you willing to gossip with him, he always asks if any others like himself have been by. There'd be no way to prevent someone coming along later to ask about him, see?''

Longarm nodded, but said, ''Those two found alive but dying knew they'd done wrong, and likely knew somebody had been tipped off about the jade they'd been hoping to sell in Frisco on the sly. We can backtrack to where they might have found any once we see whether I'm full of hot air or on to something.''

Little Pete said, ''Since you brought that up, I've been meaning to ask how you suddenly became such an expert on the Chinese jade market. Who told you all this shit about sneaky prospectors pocketing lumps of prime jade in the first place?''

Longarm said, ''You and those two dying Chinese. Or mayhaps I should say *yu* and those two dying Chinese.''

Little Pete stared blankly at first. Then, since he was fluent in both Cantonese and English, whether a word sounded exactly the same in either, he suddenly laughed and said, ''Of course! It's so simple when you remember *yu* means *jade* at Fong the jeweler's!''

Longarm nodded and said. ''They both allowed they'd been warned they might be killed by *yu*, which makes no sense to an American who hears *yu* as *you*. But let's not worry about all those Chinese done in by *yu* or the love of *yu*. What's done is done, and we still have to catch the animal, not vegetable or mineral, behind all this bloody bullshit!''

Chapter 21

It was the earlier of the two night boats that offered a killer the most darkness on the way to Frisco. So Longarm boarded it as soon as they let down the gangplank, carrying his heavily laden McClellan and wearing his .44-40 openly for the time being.

The purser stationed nearby stopped him and started to say he'd have to check those guns. But then he recognized Longarm from the earlier voyage and said, "Oh, you're one of Marshal Seaforth's men. Do you need help with that load, sir?"

Longarm allowed it was more awkward than heavy, and said he knew the way, even though, this trip, they'd put him in another stateroom.

It was close enough to one he'd had earlier. He stored his saddle and possibles, hung his gunbelt in the closet, and ambled back out on deck to light up and see who else he had to worry about.

None of the white folks coming aboard matched any wanted fliers he'd read recently, and he knew Little Pete, one deck down, would know better about which Chinese coming aboard might make trouble.

It was too early to compare notes with his Oriental ace in the hole. He smoked by the port rail until they cast off, and then he strolled around to the starboard promenade to watch the sun go down as they steamed south at a good clip with the current. A young gal, who'd have been prettier if her teeth had stuck out less, shyly asked him if those mountains off to the west were the Sierra Nevadas.

He gravely told her that was the Coast Range, even though she likely knew that already. It was sort of a shame he wouldn't be able to tell her more about the wonders of the West. Kissing a pretty bucktoothed gal could be sort of interesting.

But it wouldn't have been fair to either of them to start anything he wouldn't be able to finish. So he ticked his hat brim to her, and would have gone back to the main salon if she hadn't come tagging after him.

He found a stairwell just aft of the paddle box, and went down to the cargo deck instead, knowing she wouldn't dare follow. He meant to go right back up and get to that bar from the port side. So he was on his way between the engine room bulkhead and a cargo bin when Little Pete caught up with him and remarked, "Longarm, you are full of shit. I went over your list with some of my own boys earlier. Wong Lai and Gum How, the two that accused *yu* of killing them, had been up around a couple of the old gold camps, but after that it gets silly. Gum How, the boy those hunters fished out of the water, had been betting heavy in a fan-tan game aboard this very vessel and he'd lost his whole poke. I mean a *gold* poke. *All* of it. Zero. Flat broke! At least two hours before somebody knifed him in the back and rolled him over the rail!"

Longarm shrugged and suggested, "He was knifed and tossed overboard by somebody who has it in for poverty-stricken Sons of Han? Who's to say he wasn't packing some more valuable jade he didn't dare gamble with?"

Little Pete started to say Longarm just didn't know how fan-tan was played among his own kind. But he was sharp for such a squirt, and decided, "Betting a thousand-dollar lump of jade you'd never told your tong about *could* take years off a man's life. But now we come to the good part. We have eighteen Cantonese aboard right now, all told. Only eleven of them have been anywhere near the Sierra Nevadas, and only one out of the whole bunch has been prospecting near one of those gold camps on your list. A place called Alligator Rock.''

Longarm nodded and said, ''Alligators are the right color. So why am I full of shit?''

Little Pete replied, ''We just searched him. His name is Sung Wu. He's a Sen Suey. He didn't want us to search him. So now we have to explain those bruises to the Sen Sueys.''

''You didn't find any jade on him?'' Longarm asked.

Little Pete grimaced and confided, ''He had less than three full ounces of gold dust and barely enough pocket change to see him home.''

Longarm shrugged and said, ''A rock can look like an alligator without being jadeite. This book I read says the few jadeite outcrops rooted in bedrock are way off in Wyoming. Most of *all* the jade ever found was found as boulders down to cobbles, in streambeds, on either side of a big pond. This one book suggests nephrite and jadeite are both formed in pockets of softer rock that washes away to free loose lumps of jade that just lay about until somebody comes along.''

Little Pete sniffed and said, ''Sung Wu says he didn't even pan too much *gold* around Alligator Rock. What do we do now?''

Longarm said, ''We keep our eyes peeled. We have a long night boat ride ahead of us, and if I knew what might happen we wouldn't have to keep our eyes peeled.''

Little Pete was young. He protested, ''Damn it, Longarm, we've drawn a bad hand this trip. There's only one man aboard who could have been packing jade and he ain't packing jade!''

''Or so he says,'' Longarm pointed out, sweeping the surrounding nooks and crannies with his gaze as he dryly suggested, "A man could hide many a fair-sized green potato aboard a steamboat if he was of a mind to. I just now hide away a whole saddle and my regular gun rig. Anybody searching me right now might find a small double derringer and a snub-nosed .445 on me. But they'd have to know where I stowed my .44-40 if they wanted to admire it."

Little Pete said, "Oh, shit, now you want an Easter egg hunt and we're not even Christians! If I was dead sure the boy was holding out, we have ways of making him talk, and the Sen Suey would be pleased to know we'd worked such a big fibber over. But I'm *not* dead sure, and you don't tell someone's tong boss you worked him over without one hell of a reason, see?"

Longarm said he followed the kid's drift, and headed back up to the promenade deck for some beer and grub.

As he was salting a boiled egg at the free-lunch counter, a familiar but far from friendly voice growled in his ear, "I thought I told you you were off the case, Deputy Long!"

Longarm turned to smile at Marshal Seaforth, who didn't seem to be smiling back, and said, "Evening, Tavish. Since I ain't working for you, I don't have to address you by your title, do I?"

"What are you doing aboard this vessel?" the older lawman demanded. "I thought I told you to go upstream or down and keep going!"

Longarm bit off some egg and washed it down with beer as the older man stewed. Then he said, "It's a free country. If you feel I'm in violation of some federal statute, why don't you try and arrest me?"

Seaforth reddened and blustered, "I don't think I like your tone at all and I mean to tell Billy Vail the same!"

Longarm enjoyed some more free lunch and calmly replied, "I don't give a shit. My conscience is clean, and I ain't ashamed to own up to a thing I've done or said to your nephew's widow. She told me nobody would take her to that church social because they were all afraid of Miwok Mason. Whether she had that right or not, Miwok was a pain in the ass as well as a public danger. I shot him in the ass as he was out to kill me in one of his crazy fits. You told me how you felt about that. So let's say no more about it. Would you like to hear about a notion I just had about the more serious bloodshed aboard these riverboats?''

Seaforth snapped that they weren't talking, and added that Longarm had best get off in Frisco and take the train home from there, if he knew what was good for him.

Longarm tried some of the famous California cheddar cheese next.

It was good, but too filling to eat all night. So Longarm went out on the promenade and found a deck chair near the port stern to settle down a spell. It was dark and he was working on his third or fourth smoke when that buck-toothed brunette caught up with him, sat down beside him uninvited, and asked if he was married.

Longarm gravely replied, ''Not to Christian thinking, ma'am. But my squaws and me have been together many a happy year. Lord love 'em.''

She gasped, ''Squaws? Plural? You admit to being a squaw man living in a state of sin with more than one such savage redskin?''

He shook his head and calmly told her, ''Winona and Shunkaweya would never go for that, ma'am. They'd scratch each other's eyes out if I lived with them both under the same roof. But fortunately I travel, and so I have one squaw over in Cheyenne and keep the younger one in Frisco, where we're headed.''

She sprang up and lit out before he could ask what sort of sin *she* preferred to live in. The steamer churned on, and he caught himself nodding off. So he got back up and prowled the promenade a dozen odd times before he met up with that purser, smoking alone near the taffrail near the head of a literal ladderway up to the Texas or down to the cargo deck. Longarm howdied the somewhat older man in a dark blazer and peaked cap. Then he asked how far down they were, seeing it was black as a bitch out, with the moon still hiding behind the high mountains off to the east. The purser said they'd have moonlight to spare by the time they had to navigate the tricky channels of the delta. He might have answered some other questions Longarm was fixing to ask about the crew if Marshal Seaforth hadn't barged in to tell Longarm to beat it.

Longarm would have pointed out it was a free country and he'd paid good money for the right to walk the public promenade. But before he could, the three of them heard a fusillade of gunfire from below.

"Cover me!" snapped Marshal Seaforth as he forgot his personal feelings to grab the ladder rails and vanish from sight while gunsmoke roiled up through the hatch.

Longarm tore after him, grabbed the same steel rails, and slid down them to turn at the bottom and take in the wild scene.

As best he could make out through swirling smoke in tricky light, the older lawman who'd proceeded him was looming, gun in hand, above three figures sprawled across the stern deck. One denim-clad figure lay facedown in a spreading puddle of blood with a knife hilt sprouting between his shoulder blades. A bigger white man lay spread-eagle on his back in bell-bottoms and a pea jacket with a big Walker Colt conversion on the deck beside his head. Little Pete was sprawled in the scuppers with his own Le Mat Duplex gripped weakly in one hand.

The purser was coming down behind him as Longarm thoughtfully knelt and pulled up his pants leg to quietly ask which one Seaforth had shot.

The older lawman snorted, "Don't be an asshole. You heard the last shots from up above. It looks as if one of these birds caught the other stabbing yon Chinaman. So they shot it out and nobody won!"

Longarm cleared the grips of his Webley Bulldog as he stared over at the small limp form of Little Pete and muttered, "Damn it, kid. I told you to keep your eyes peeled!"

Marshal Seaforth bent over the bigger man Little Pete

had downed and chortled, "Hot shit! This one's gutshot but still alive! Maybe now we'll get some answers or he won't get any laudanum to ease the discomforts of a slow but sure demise. The first thing we want to make sure of is who the poor boy might be."

Standing near the foot of the ladder, the purser said in a conversational tone, "He's one of my baggage hands."

Then he shot Marshal Seaforth in the back.

As the older lawman fell forward to sprawl facedown with his hat and gun closer to the dead Chinese, the purser swung the smoking muzzle of his .38-caliber Colt Lightning to cover Longarm, snarling, "I'll kill you if you try to draw. I might let you live if you'd care to roll all four of them over the side for me right now!"

Longarm knew the treacherous bastard was lying. They could both hear running footsteps up above. There was no way in hell for a man to draw a gun from his boot, aim, and fire in the time he had to work with staring straight into a gun muzzle.

But he was dead either way. So he had to try, and he wasn't at all surprised when the purser fired first.

But there was something about having one's head explode like a sledgehammered watermelon that threw a man's aim off considerably.

The purser's shot missed Longarm by inches as his peaked cap flew high with gobs of hairy scalp and frothy brain tissue. Then Longarm put some .445 lead in his chest to bounce him off the steel ladder.

As the thoroughly shot-up purser collapsed in a sincerely dead pile at the foot of the ladder, Longarm turned to see Little Pete reclining on one elbow, with fresh smoke rising from the central shotgun barrel of the double-gaited Le Mat and a sickly grin on his sallow face.

Those footsteps were milling in confusion up above, and somebody was calling in Cantonese from the forward cargo deck. Little Pete called out in the same lingo. Then he nod-

171

ded at Longarm to report they had everything under control on that deck.

Longarm said, "I'm pleased to see the earlier reports of your death were premature. Let's see how everyone else made out."

He kicked the gutshot baggage hand's Walker across the deck to the hatchet man, and hunkered down over Marshal Seaforth to ask him how he felt.

The older lawman muttered, "What happened? Why did you shoot me? I didn't think you were *that* serious about Mairi!"

Longarm pulled Seaforth's coat and shirttails up to expose the wound near the spine, growling, "Hang a wreath on your nose. Your brain just died. It looks like your floating rib stopped the ball and it just knocked the wind out of you. You'll likely live, and you owe it to the silly-looking Chinaman with the silly-looking gun yonder."

He saw Little Pete was on his hands and knees now, shaking his head like a bird dog coming ashore as he marveled, "By *T'ien*, it feels like a mule kicking you when you get hit in the chest by a .45-40!"

Longarm said, "You ought to lie down some more if you've been shot in the breast, Little Pete. What's the story here?"

Little Pete said, "I caught him in the act of stabbing Sung Wu over there. I don't know why. I told you Sung Wu had no jade on him. But I was watching him, as you told me to, and I made the mistake of trying to take that big bastard alive so he could tell us what made him so mean to us squint-eyed rascals. He pulled that horse pistol and fired first. The rest you know."

Longarm snorted, "The hell you say! How come you look so chipper after getting shot with a .45-40?"

Little Pete put his baby cannon away in his shoulder rig as he got to his full height, which wasn't much, and proceeded to unbutton his smoke-stained ruffled shirt, shyly saying he didn't do this for *all* the boys.

172

Then he opened his shirt to show Longarm the gleaming fine-meshed chain-mail vest he'd been wearing under it, and asked, "Satisfied?"

Longarm nodded wearily and said, "It's about time I got some straight answers around here. Now button up and let me do all the talking!"

Chapter 22

An undetermined number of hatchet men supervised by Little Pete and the four junior deputies Longarm took command of, with Marshal Seaforth's blessing, had the steamer secured in no time, and her skipper said they had *his* blessing too.

Marshal Seaforth had been right about that laudanum. There were two doctors on board, and not a thing anyone could do for the gutshot baggage hand and killer but dose him with enough of the same to ease his pain and loosen his tongue. So they soon had another baggage hand and the purser's mate handcuffed under guard, lest howling Chinese pay them back in pain and suffering before the State of California got to try them for murder and hang them high.

It was more important to Longarm that he'd be able to put together a more detailed official report. He seemed stuck with the job once they got to Frisco and shoved Marshal Seaforth in the hospital along with the slowly recovering Sally Speedwell née Sullivan and the slowly dying mate off the S.S. *Queensland*.

Longarm was just getting the hang of things when the nearby San Francisco District Court relieved him. That was what they called it when they put a higher-ranking local man in charge, relieving you.

Longarm didn't care. He'd already been fighting with the navy over who had proper jurisdiction and, as he'd later confess to Billy Vail, he hadn't been too certain they had no call to horn in. They were sure in better shape to chase after crooks at sea.

Leaving the local muck-a-mucks and reporters to sort things out, he boarded the Oakland ferry the next Friday morning to head back for Denver and less cussing and swearing.

He knew he'd be damned if he did and damned if he didn't send word about her uncle to Mairi Seaforth by river steamer, and the long way around by faster railroad tracks got him to Sacramento in time to connect with the same eastbound Central Pacific Pullman. So why shop for trouble? Experience had shown that a man met up with all the trouble he'd ever need whether he shopped for it or not.

As if to prove that point, Longarm had no sooner settled down with a magazine in his hired compartment when, before the train had made it as far as the foothills, there came a timid knock on the sliding door and Longarm rose to open it and stare thunderstruck at the very gal he'd gone clean around the Sacramento-San Joaquin delta to avoid.

"May I come in?" asked Mairi Seaforth demurely, even as she barged in from the companionway in her travel duster and straw sunbonnet. She put her carpetbag down inside the doorway about the time Longarm told her to. He shut the door after her with an uneasy glance out into the thankfully empty companionway.

The bunk bed along the windows offered the only comfortable seat, and was no more shocking than the hardwood lid of the built-in crapper by the sink, as soon as you studied on it. So he sat her down beside him as he soberly asked what in blue thunder she was doing there.

She said she was starting over in Omaha, where there were all sorts of opportunities for a gal who knew how to play pianos or typewriters and wasn't really that old yet.

175

Longarm asked, "What about your property back in Reedport, ma'am?"

She shrugged and said, "I just gave it back to the bank that held a mortgage on it to begin with. The equity check they gave me ought to see me to Omaha and last me until I'm on my feet and truly free again, thanks to *you*, Custis."

To which Longarm could only reply, "Aw, mush. I spanked that bully because he needed spanking, and as you said yourself, Miwok Mason was only part of your struggle with lonesome, Miss Mairi."

She nodded soberly and said, "I know. Uncle Tavish told me nobody but himself would ever pay court to me in Reedport, that same evening he drove you out of town after your fight with Miwok!"

Longarm grimaced and said, "Well, the last time I saw him he was nursing a bullet wound in a hospital bed. So we'll say no more about whether I was chased or just left politely. His feelings ain't all that hard to fathom, Miss Mairi. Heaps of big brothers, uncles, and even old dads have mixed emotions when it comes to other men and the innocent charms no other dirty rascal has any right to enjoy as long as *they* ain't allowed to."

She grimaced and said, "Uncle Tavish seemed to feel he was allowed to. He pointed out he was only my uncle by marriage to a late nephew and so it wouldn't really be incest, the beast!"

Longarm nodded soberly and said, "He was right, as far as the law reads, Miss Mairi. I reckon, like a lot of dirty old men, he couldn't see how it might strike a gal young enough to be his daughter when he suddenly came at her acting way less fatherly."

Mairi repressed a shudder and confided, "The thought of kissing my own father or my one real uncle doesn't make my flesh crawl half as much! I was happy with Duncan Seaforth. I was *very* happy, and we had a good marriage with a lot of . . . warmth between us. But it was Duncan I fell in love with and lost. I'd always wondered why his

176

uncle made me feel so . . . uneasy, until your showdown with Miwok Mason brought things to a head.''

Longarm started to say something in defense of old Tavish Seaforth, seeing he was a pal of old Billy Vail. Then he recalled how mean the old fart had talked to *him* more than once, and said, ''I was hoping you'd see old Tavish was indulging a bully who never had a chance with you, lest some swain who *might* have had a chance with you showed up on your doorstep to carry you off to some church social or Grange dance.''

She gravely asked why he hadn't said so back in Reedport. He just as gravely told her it hadn't been for him to say.

Reading the smoke in her hazel eyes the only way a man could read them, Longarm told her, ''You're a woman grown. So I don't have to talk to you as if you were a foolish virgin, Miss Mairi. I reckon I know what it has to feel like to sleep alone a lot after a happy marriage to a healthy young rider. But it was up to you and you alone to do something about such itchings.''

''Are you saying you were never tempted to . . . scratch my back, Custis?''

Longarm laughed sheepishly and confessed, ''I'm a man, and any woman who's ever known men in the Biblical sense knows how easy it is to tempt us, Miss Mairi. But you were a respectable widow woman with a reputation to consider, and there was a possessive uncle by marriage I had to consider as well, see?''

She must have. She untied her sunbonnet and tossed it aside as she said, ''We're not in Reedport any more. We're alone aboard this train with nobody to consider but ourselves and our own desires, Custis. So why don't you draw the blinds before we shock passing strangers in broad daylight?''

He said, ''Miss Mairi, I'll be getting off at Cheyenne, and even if I wasn't, you'd find more future with a tumbleweed blowing in the wind!''

She began to unbutton her duster as she softly said, "I know. That doesn't give us much time, does it?"

Of course, in point of fact, they had plenty of time, and the sun had barely set outside when they just had to stop to catch their breath and finish undressing after what Mairi swore had been her first fuck since she'd lost her true love and more of her youth than she cared to study on. Longarm wasn't lying when he told her *he* hadn't had anyone better for a coon's age. They *all* felt as swell the first few times a man was in them, bless their ever-slightly-different charms.

Hers had copper-colored hair all over, he saw, when he struck them a light for a shared cheroot in the rumbling gloom of the now-darkened compartment. The rest of her was almost white as cream, save for where the sun had freckled her pretty face and a sort of V halfway down between her breasts. He was pleased to find them about the right size and shape for her long and lanky build. Unlike both versions of La Strega, Mairi had a natural earthy temperament, and a man could just love her up indefinitely without being bitched at to stop or go faster. You had to feel sorry for old Duncan Seaforth, getting himself killed with such a comfortable bed partner waiting for him in vain.

He didn't say so, lest he make her feel sad. She seemed to like it with his half-limp organ-grinder still inside her as they lay spooned with their heads together, taking turns with his cheroot.

He was enjoying a drag when Mairi sighed and said, "In a way it's just as well you'll be getting off at Cheyenne and I'll be going on alone, Custis. A girl could get too used to this, and mayhaps *I'd* as soon tumbleweed in the wind a while before I settle down again. Time's cruel teeth give women so few years to ... tumbleweed, and there have been nights I cursed my poor Duncan for having used up so many of mine as a happily married woman. Does that shock you?"

178

He thrust a tad deeper lest it fall out of her tight sweet-smelling slit, and replied, "I just now said I followed your drift, kitten. Time ain't all that generous to us menfolk, once you study all the gals we won't ever in this world have time to even dance with. You'll feel way better about the next lucky cuss you settle down with if you have some good dirty fun first."

She said she meant to, and added, "I'm so glad you came along and solved everything for everybody in the delta, Custis. I was stuck in a rut and nobody could solve those murders that kept happening and happening until, within just a few short days, you put everything right! How did you ever get so old and wise without losing your horny feelings, Custis?"

He began to feel horny in her again as he snuggled closer and told her, "Aw, I ain't older and wiser than the lawmen who were already on the scene. I just got lucky. I'd have never brought matters to a head for you in Reedport if Miwok Mason had simply behaved his fool self. As for what seemed too complicated a case of river piracy for others, it had me mighty confused as well at first. Then I met up with this professional sorceress who showed me the light, even as she was out to befuddle me totally."

Mairi arched her spine and purred, "Ooh, *nice*! You say a *sorceress* told you what was really going on aboard those night boats, darling?"

He said, "Not in so many words. She didn't know any more than the rest of us. But like I said, she set out to befuddle me, and for just a spell she had me wondering because what I seemed to be seeing was so unbelievable. Once I figured out what I *was* seeing, it was a childishly simple trick. It was only two different gals claiming to be one."

Mairi twitched her warm wet innards teasingly as she asked which witch he'd found the tightest. Longarm said, "That's neither here nor there and I'll never tell on *you*.

179

My point was that adding one and one to make one can confound one."

Mairi began to move under him languidly as she indulged in another joy of good sex, which was good talk in bed. She asked him what those two spooky gals had to do with river pirates.

Longarm rolled her facedown and got astride her long legs to do her deeper from behind with his balls between her smooth thighs as he answered conversationally, "We thought we were after one gang who were after white and Chinese passengers on both decks. As long as we kept that impossible picture in our fool heads, nobody we had any call to suspect seemed possible. Neither bunch knew what the other was up to. But by working at cross-purpose they tended to alibi one another. The word *alibi* comes from Lawyer Latin and means you were somewhere else at the time of the crime. Neither gang was slick enough to *plan* any really clever excuses. Either one would have been caught in no time if they'd been preying on passengers without unintentional help."

She asked if she could turn over and finish more romantically. So he let her, and she sure felt tailor-made for his own muscular body as he humped her harder till they came again like old pals who'd been together a spell but hadn't started to fight over trifles yet. He never said so. A man had to watch what he said to a lady while he was laying her. They had the habit of remembering but twisting words said in moments of intimacy when it felt as if the war was over.

As he lay there soaking with half his weight on his own courteous elbows, Longarm felt safer explaining, "According to the purser's mate, who never really killed nobody and hopes to save his own neck, it all began innocent enough, with just a few Chinese taking the purser's good advice and storing lumps of jade and extra pokes of color in his safe. It took the purser and his pals a while to figure out the Chinese who took them up on the offer were holding out on their own Chinatown grubstakers. This could get fatal if your tong ordered a random inspection on the cargo deck. So the deal was for the purser to hang on to their extra profits until they felt safe about slipping on shore with them.''

She raised both thighs to cross her shod ankles over his bare ass some more as he continued. ''A hatchet man I know is bent on collecting from a Frisco import-export firm shipping jade to China directly. They never bought any from poor but dishonest Chinee prospectors. The purser and his pals murdered them whilst their jade and color lay in the safe in the purser's cabin. An Oriental expert on such matters assured me no one man could take a wiry mining man on his guard. But it was easier for a man the victim knew as a fellow crook to draw him aside for a few private words about his jade, stick a knife in him, and roll him over the side. Then a white man no tong had ever heard of could sell the proceeds openly as his *own* gold field gleanings. The one victim who smelled a rat and made a run for it without his jade was knifed in a Barbary Coast alley to confuse us more by babbling about his jade in Cantonese. But the greedy white men who'd stabbed him clumsily and run away when a whore opened her window were just lucky, not clever by half. Next case.''

Mairi was starting to move her hips again. But she still asked him how those white passengers had been attacked in their staterooms.

He thrust in time with her as he replied, ''That never happened. Old Doc Farnsworth singled out likely shanghai victims for Silken Sally. She lured them to her place on shore, away from the docks patrolled by the police and Buckley's Lambs. We know how she drugged them to be delivered to ruthless short-handed skippers because she's been singing like a canary as she recovers from her own medicine, and the navy has been taking down a heap of names. So that's about all there really was to either case.''

Mairie sighed and said, ''Oh, pooh, I was hoping for

more cunning wheels within wheels! Whatever else can we talk about all the way to Cheyenne?''

Longarm started moving in her faster as he assured her, ''We'll think of something. Did I ever tell you about the time I was snowed in with these frisky young gals, one blanket, and not a stick of stovewood left to keep us from freezing to death?''

She laughed, and didn't sound worried as she pointed out they had the cold high country of the Sierra Nevadas ahead of them.